And Then I Woke Up

ALSO BY MALCOLM DEVLIN

Unexpected Places to Fall From, Unexpected Places to Land
You Will Grow Into Them
Engines Beneath Us

AND THEN I WOKE UP

MALCOLM DEVLIN

A TOM DOHERTY ASSOCIATES BOOK

NEW YORK

AND THEN I WOKE UP

Copyright © 2022 by Malcolm Devlin

Cover art by Samuel Araya
Cover design by Christine Foltzer

Edited by Ellen Datlow

A Tordotcom Book
Published by Tom Doherty Associates
120 Broadway
New York, NY 10271

www.tor.com

Tor® is a registered trademark of Macmillan Publishing Group, LLC.

ISBN 978-1-250-79808-4 (ebook)
ISBN 978-1-250-79807-7 (trade paperback)

First Edition: 2022

To Helen

And Then I Woke Up

Whenever I tell people what happened, I tell them it was a love story. I stand by that, even though I know when I'm done, you might disagree.

It's one of the lessons Macey taught me. Macey was my believer. Here's her picture, pass it around the group. That sceptical expression she's giving the camera? That's the look she always gave me. She once told me when you say you're going to tell people a horror story, they sit up in their chairs defensively, waiting to see you fail. When you tell them it's a love story, they relax, they open themselves wide. Macey used to write horror stories she sold as love stories. She took a certain pleasure in seeing her audience find themselves out of their depth.

When I say this is a love story, I mean this is a story about someone who believed in something impossible and beautiful and dangerous with such strength of character and devotion that they followed the thread of it all the way to the very end, no matter what the world threw at them.

Whichever way you try to tell it, that sounds like a love story to me.

1

Nobody wanted the room next to Leila's and it wasn't because when curfew came, she turned out to be a screamer. It was because she was silent.

When you've been at Ironside as long as most of us have, you'll know it's the silent ones who are the worst. That's because they're *different*. And while the mantra of Awad and the Ironside doctors is how we need to celebrate what we have in common, it's those differences—even the smallest and most trivial—that scare us the most.

The truth is, everybody gets night terrors here. Awad denies it, but I swear it's part of the cure. It's part of the process of getting better. Put your hand up if you sleep soundly every night. See? Me neither. And no wonder. Night means darkness, darkness means introspection, introspection dredges up all kinds of monsters and my god, do those bastards keep us busy until dawn.

When I was here before, I always imagined you could set a clock by some of the patients. Now I'm back, it's clear that little has changed.

Vasquez—where are you? *There* you are. Vasquez here is still in room 23 and still wakes up promptly at four each morning. You do! In the daytime, I'd say he was the best adjusted of all of us, but during the night? Well, he doesn't scream exactly. He *huffs* and *haws* like he's been winded by something heavy hitting his chest. I'm not passing judgement, man. I'm only saying.

Who else do we have? Schonnel whimpers, Guardia squeaks, Sizemore can't keep still. The walls in this place are only a few millimetres of chipboard, cordoning off what had once been the school gymnasium into our grid of narrow little cells. Half-a-dozen rooms in the east corridor are full of cries and shouts and screams. Awad said living here is like living next to a waterfall. To begin with, the noise seems impossible to ignore, but the longer you stay, the less you notice it, the more it registers as part of your sense of the place. Once you're used to it, having it taken away becomes the bigger distraction.

Leila didn't make a peep after dark.

"I have a daughter," Sizemore told me. "When she was a baby, I'd spend my nights watching her sleep. Sometimes babies are quiet. Sometimes, they're *really* quiet. Sometimes you really have to look at them to prove to yourself they're still breathing. And on those nights, I couldn't breathe until she breathed first.

"When I'm in the room next to that woman? My god,

I'm holding my breath until I'm blue in the face. I'm not going to go through that again."

So that's how I got the room next to Leila's and I swear it sounded as though she drew a breath when the lights went off and didn't release it until sun-up. There was a strange and disquieting quality to her silence, but it didn't bother me the way it did Sizemore and everyone else. It was seductive. Like the patch of darkness you can see through an open window that you keep staring at because you have an idea *something* might appear there.

I'd been at Ironside for nearly two years by then. Leila had been there for about six months. She was a small and wiry figure, lean and agile, the same jagged knot of nervous energy marking most of the recently cured. When she came into a room, limping on her bad leg, everyone would notice. Her being would flare like a flashbulb. We'd turn to see her hovering in the doorway, judging her exits should she need to make an escape.

She'd been in isolation for several months before she was given the run of the place with the rest of us. A month or so longer than most. For special cases like hers, the gentle escalation from one-to-one supervision to everyone-in-it-together was given more time, more care.

We knew her road here had been tough. The Ironside staff still had her on a watch list; the red light of the security camera mounted in the corner of her room never blinked. She was fitted with slip-on shoes, happy pills, no belts, no braces. They treated her like she could shatter at any moment.

Her silence extended to group sessions. She was watchful, and we could see she was listening as we talked through our horror stories. It was clear her understanding of reality had dawned, but it was still incomplete. The inevitable, clanging *acceptance* was still due.

All of this was *normal*, Doctor Awad reminded us with his usual patience. New arrivals needed time to acclimatise to how the world had shaped itself around them.

"It's like she's woken up," he said. "Her dream-life has ended abruptly. We have to show her this is a *good* thing, the *best* outcome. We have to show her *this* is the world worth living in no matter what might have happened. No matter what she might be responsible for."

Group sessions are all about that kind of support. We each have stories, and we each sit up straight in our chairs when someone else takes their turn to tell theirs. We've all done terrible, terrible things. We were monsters once, and although we are not anymore, we know we remain unforgiven to everyone who isn't in the group.

Whatever Leila was going through, hers was merely one of a multitude of similar stories and we needed to prove to her we'd all been through the same grind. Even though she hadn't shared her story with us yet, we had a very good idea what kind of story it was.

The thing about new people in the group was that it was another opportunity for the rest of us to tell our own stories again. We're hungry for fresh listeners, because the more you tell your own story, the more it makes sense to you, and as Awad delights in pointing out, the more the cure works.

"You keep telling yourself what happened until you believe it."

He isn't wrong. Really, he isn't.

So, we took turns confessing before the newcomer. Weeping before her; accepting everyone's embraces so she could see how—in *this* place—none of us were judged for the atrocities we had committed when we weren't ourselves.

Isn't it beautiful how stories can work like that? The subtle way they help the teller, the subversive way they reach the listener, how they creep inside you like waking dreams.

"After the narrative," Awad says, "it's important to learn to trust stories again."

Leila would sit quietly on her chair like you lot are doing right now, but her hands would be clasping and unclasping on her lap as she listened, patient as a rock and enduring us all.

"Leila?" Awad's tone was a gentle, exploratory question in itself. Leila would shake her head, a quick, curtailed, and silent answer.

"Not today, then," Awad would say. "That's all, everyone."

Leila ate meals alone. She would carry her tray to the end of the table near the broad window overlooking what had once been the school's playground. The fences along the road had been built up high, so there wasn't much view to speak of, but she would gaze outward, where the nearby gum trees and jacarandas would rise above the fence line in vivid plumes.

The rest of us wondered what she was looking for.

"She's looking for an escape route," Sizemore said. "It's like she's still infected. She's a caged animal looking for a way out."

"She's looking at the sky," Guardia said. "When you're infected, you never see how it really looks. How beautiful the clouds can be."

"She's looking at the basketball court," Linden said. "Wondering where they've moved all the kids. She's sad for them."

After a month of living with the ghost of her, I waited until Leila took her seat at dinnertime, then I went to join her. Sitting across the table, a couple of chairs down. I saw her tense up, her knuckles whitening around her plastic cutlery.

"Listen," I said, my voice low, "I can fuck off if you want me to. You only have to say the word. Or give me the finger, or the stink eye or whatever makes you comfortable. I'm not going to say or do anything more than keep you company. Only if you'll have it, mind."

She didn't say a word, she didn't even look at me, and so I stayed.

It was a cheap move, strong-arming my way into her personal space until she became used to me. Linden had done the same when I first arrived, and while it felt like a long road, we got on in the end. The truth is, I saw Leila on her own and I wanted to throw her a rope.

It took a while, but the signs were there that Leila was warming to me. She'd cast me a shy smile when I joined her at mealtimes, a nod when we crossed paths in the corridor or on the way to the washroom. We were neighbours by then. I hoped she'd seen me switching rooms with Sizemore as an act of kindness rather than anything opportune.

The first time I heard her speak was nearly a month after I first started sitting at her table in the canteen. I was in the common room, the old school assembly hall, sitting in the strip of grey light that spilled through the tall, frosted-glass windows. I was a little down. I'd been thinking of Macey, and that always sent me into a spiral. So, there I was, leafing through the deck of photographs I keep in my pocket when Leila approached me.

"Family?" she said. Her voice was soft, but her accent had sharpened the edges of it.

I shook my head, putting them away. I was torn. I wanted to have something to talk to her about, but I wasn't quite ready to talk about *them*. Not away from the safety of the group.

"No."

"Your . . . people, then?" The term didn't quite fit right and we both knew it.

I nodded anyway.

"You got any yourself?" I said, realising how forward it sounded only once I had said it out loud. To her credit she didn't take offence and only shook her head a fraction.

"The doctors aren't going that route," she said.

I didn't push it any further.

She glanced to the window and sighed deeply.

"I hate the rain," she said.

It was a cloudy day. The closeness of the temperature suggested a storm was due. For now, the threat of rain was only present in the heaviness of the air. I said some nonsense about how the grass seemed to appreciate it, how it looked more verdant than it often did at that time of year.

Leila shot me a look that surprised me. I had only

known her quiet and closed off. But the meekness appeared to have been painted-on. Now her eyebrows were arched and her expression was sardonic, broadly amused.

"I know they preach about seeing all sides here," she said. "But shaming me for hating the rain is a bit much, don't you think?"

I blushed and backtracked. "I've been here a while," I said.

Her smile was small, but it was a smile, nonetheless.

"How long's a while?"

I told her and she whistled.

"Are you hoping they'll give you a job if you stay?" she said. "Janitor, maybe?"

I laughed, and the reaction seemed to shake her. The mask slipped back up and her eyes shifted downward. Her cheeks flushed, as though she was embarrassed she had given herself away.

When she spoke again, her tone was more delicate, a little forced.

"Nowhere else to go, huh?" she said.

I shook my head, the truth of her words passing like the shadow of a storm cloud.

Macey once told me the problem with the truth was that it was so poorly written. Given the choice, the pleasantly told lie is always more seductive. That's why religion is so potent, she said. Why history and science are still considered up for debate. Myth is more appealing than verified truth because the grey areas between the facts can still be used against us.

"Spence?" Leila said. I think it was the first time she used my name, and she wasn't the first who had used it like a prompt to jog me back to the present.

"Sorry," I said. "Nowhere to go. What about you?"

She didn't even blink in surprise.

"We'll see," she said.

Less than a month later she told me she was leaving, and it was clear this was a decision she'd made some time ago. She'd simply been waiting for an opportunity she could use to convince herself it was time.

On the day Leila told me she wanted to escape, the common room television was showing a daytime magazine show. The sound was off as usual, and the day supervisor patrolling the room was armed with the remote control so they could switch over to the cartoons whenever a news bulletin came on.

These days, what's broadcast is carefully controlled. The news is tempered, shorn of opinion; dramas are kept calm and easygoing, the stakes have been lowered, and whatever they do show is calibrated to be much less intense. It's not *censorship,* we're assured, it's simply a form of moderation, *for our own good.* Nothing divisive, nothing to make people angry, nothing to make people scared. At Ironside, we get even less. A shadow of a shadow of the media we once knew. We get fashion tips and decorating tutorials; we get kids' TV shows; we get the shopping channel with its endless Tupperware and paste jewellery.

Funny, isn't it? You tell yourself that when the world ends, all of that nonsense will dry up. It'll be like a purge of the banal, and all the trivia of the world will be the first down the plughole. But no, the same old shit floats to the top without needing us to be there to witness it. Yesterday, the highlight of my day was seeing a group of junior chefs competing to see who could make the best cheeseburger; this morning there was a silent music video from a singer-songwriter with a furrowed brow.

It's all very *safe* and *reassuring.* Nobody's going to go crazy and shoot up a roomful of people because of a knitting demonstration.

At least, I don't think they will.

Logic might tell you it would be safer not to have a television at all in a room full of people who fell for the bullshit of the narrative the first time. My own suspicion is the television is not there for our own entertainment; it's another tool Ironside uses to test the cure.

Think about it. When the narrative has taken hold, it brings with it a constricting of focus; a tendency to only see what is perceived to be true at the expense of everything else. If any one of us were to look at the television and see it to be blank, or see only static or distortion, or a mass of images their brain refuses to process? Well, the security here is trained to spot that kind of "not seeing." It's a particular skill to notice someone who isn't noticing properly, and you can imagine what happens then. The burlier supers—Danvers, maybe, or Thorn—they'll come waltzing in, two-abreast through those rattling double doors, and they'll spirit the poor fucker away to the observation rooms in the south wing.

Although we're constantly being reassured relapses are rare, it would be nonsense to say they don't happen. The infection is never really gone. It isn't communicable, but at best it's dormant. It's worked around, understood.

You might have heard of Rennet. Big guy, ginger whiskers. He used to work on a poultry farm, and his hands used to clench and unclench when he thought no one was looking. This wasn't like the way Leila's hands moved during groups—hers moved as though she was trying to get blood flowing, trying to find something to hold onto. Rennet looked like he was still throttling the livestock, day-in, day-out.

He'd been having a bad few weeks in group—the

warning signs are always there if you give them time afterward. Contempt for someone else's horror story was a red flag, so was muttering under your breath as though there's no one else who can hear what you're saying. We all knew the supers had him back on their watch list. Then, one day, in the common room, he went completely silent and still for a few hours. When he finally looked up, the gleam was back in his eye.

He started screaming. His eyes were so wide I could see the mesh of red from across the room. There was something *animal* about that scream, the furious squawk of a cage full of birds in a blind panic. By the time the supers caught up with him, he'd already punched Vasquez square in the face, sent him sprawling across the floor. He was throwing chairs at the windows to try and break his way out. God, though! You should have seen it! He was *bouncing* the things off the glass, he nearly knocked himself out in the process. It would have been funny, if only . . .

Well. The racket he made when they were steering him out of the room? I've never heard anyone sound so terrified.

The common room is a big place—high ceilings, lots of room for air. But it's usually humid in here, and with all of us milling about, the atmosphere has a certain thickness to it. Rennet, the poor bastard, had shat himself by the time the supers had a hold of him, and I swear to you, it took nearly a half-hour before the stench of it permeated every corner. Any sympathy we'd had was qualified by the smell he left us with.

He did come back, though. Rennet. Months later, this was. He was steered back into the common room, looking sheepish and drawn. His face was hollow and glistening; that shock of red hair shaved down to a military buzz cut. He looked as though the fear in him had halved his size during his absence. Vasquez acted all jovial with him, talking to him as though nothing had happened. His eye had healed up pretty well, but when Rennet looked at him, it was as though he only saw scar tissue and he was inconsolable.

You've almost certainly heard what happened to him next. Don't ask me how he did it, but he managed to electrocute himself. This was two or three weeks later. He smashed his way into a fuse box in the east corridor and wired himself up to it or something. I don't know all the details. I do remember he knocked the power out in the east wing and left most of us in darkness for few hours while the supers dealt with what was left of him.

On the day Leila decided to make her escape, the supervisor was Tully. She was doing her rounds as normal, and as she passed us, she gestured to the television with the tip of her pen.

"What's that on the screen?" she said. "What do you see now?"

When she was gone, Leila nudged me in the ribs.

"She forgot to switch out the news," she said. "Look."

I looked up and got a glimpse of a typical studio set-up. A well-presented newsreader with a prim expression and a ticker feed running along the foot of the screen. Across the room, Tully recognised her mistake and the cartoons took over.

"Anything good?" I said. It didn't seem enough to get excited about. A ghost of television past. When I turned to Leila, I saw her head was cocked and her frown had deepened. "What was it?" I said. "What did they say?"

She jumped as though I had startled her and glanced at me again.

"Something to do with the infected," she said. "It says there's a gang of them out to the south. Knocking about near the wind turbines. I think it might have been a warning, you know?"

I didn't, not precisely, but I could guess. Perhaps the news really did broadcast warnings of gangs of infected in a similar way they forecast the weather and the pollen count.

I made some joke about it. Weatherman voice: Infected sighted here, here, and here. Dress accordingly and plan different route. Leila ignored me and I went quiet, feeling foolish.

"Are you alright?" I said, too late, perhaps to make a difference if she wasn't.

When she nodded, her smile was brave.

"Oh yes," she said. "It's nothing. Really. Nothing at all."

If my time in the facility has taught me anything, it's when people insist nothing is wrong, it's a lie to buy them time to process their situation. Something was clearly troubling her, and I didn't want to press the issue. Leila had only recently started talking. She still hadn't spoken up in group, and it really wasn't my place to push her further, when opening wasn't something she took to easily.

I'd once asked her how she got her limp, and she had stared at me as though from beneath a thundercloud.

"I got bit," she said, and that served me right. I backed off.

This time, I said nothing. Leila didn't talk much, and when she did speak, she mostly spoke only to me. It was a delicate connection, but for all its ups and downs, it felt worth preserving.

If you like, you could say I let her get away with it. There would be time for her story and the timetable was hers to define, not mine.

———

Later that night, hours after the lights had gone out, she made her approach. A gentle *tap-tap-tap* from the silent room next door. I crawled out of bed, all too aware Sizemore was probably listening in on whatever I was doing.

I slipped out into the corridor and Leila was there. With a curt gesture she set off down the hallway, her bare feet quiet on the polished wooden floor.

The dining hall was empty at that time of night. Leila waited for me in the lee of one of the pillars.

"I'm leaving," she said. "I'm getting out of here."

It didn't feel like a surprise, but still, I asked her why. I could see she'd never really been comfortable at Ironside, and I think in some way I'd wanted her to understand how much her being there had helped me.

"The infected," she said. "The gang they showed on the news. There was a picture. It was only there for a moment, but I *know* them. One of them at least. The leader, I suppose, the believer. I recognised him. I'd recognise him anywhere. Val. His name is Val and—"

I could see she knew how that sounded as soon as she said it.

"I don't want to go back to them, if that's what you're thinking. I'm cured. Really, I'm cured. They'd think I'm . . . they'd kill me on sight, I know. But I want to see them. To see if they're alright. See if they're safe. Does that sound crazy to you?"

I nodded, weighing the information carefully as though it was delicate and primed to explode. A face, a name. A ghost from her infected past that—like the infection itself—she couldn't quite be completely rid of. In a sense, I envied her. I'd been easy to cure because by then I was alone. There was no one left to hold me under the influence. Would it have been different had Macey still been alive?

I spoke carefully. "Do you think," I said, "you could bring them here?"

She frowned.

"Do you think," I said, "we could cure him? Val."

It was a stupid idea, but her face brightened. She didn't need a plan that made sense, but the excuse I was offering had more logic to back it up than the one she'd concocted for herself.

"Yes!" she said. "That's what I want to do. I could bring him back here. We could make him better. Like us. You, me, Awad, everyone."

I thought of Rennet, how it might be possible to judge a relapse, but Leila was nothing like Rennet. Rennet had been loud and had fallen silent. Leila was going in the opposite direction with an enthusiasm that would have been unheard of only a week or so before. It felt to me like the symptom of a successful healing process rather than a warning sign of a failure. Just as I had my pocket full of photographs, perhaps Leila needed to see the folk she'd run with, perhaps that was the key she needed to permit herself to be fully cured.

"Out in the suburbs?" I said.

"Yes," she said. "To the south, past the forest park."

"Which suburb?"

Her eyes moved as she told me. I knew it. It was over the river and past the railway line and the sprawl of the western motorway. On the way to the wind farm up on the escarpment, which fringed the horizon like a neat row of oversized daisies.

"I'm going with you," I said.

Her eyes blazed with a brief, sharp anger.

"I don't need someone to protect me," she said.

I backtracked, my excuses woolly, trying to understand why I was offering to go at all. I liked living in Ironside. I liked the routine; I liked the company. More than anything, I liked being cured.

But I'd been there for the best part of two years, and as Leila put it when we first spoke, I had nowhere else to go.

Leila had places to go and now I desperately wanted to follow her there. I wasn't looking for someone I could protect or save. I was looking for a direction, I was looking for an open door.

"I can take care of myself," Leila said.

"I know," I said.

Her defences collapsed and her shoulders dropped. This was not a battle she needed to fight.

"Tomorrow morning, then," she said.

"Tomorrow," I agreed.

2

This is what happened.

A lot of you have heard this already, but Awad keeps saying repetition is key.

"Say it until you believe it," he says. Insisting the same techniques that open you to the narrative are the surest ways to inoculate yourself against it. So here we go again.

This is me. You'll know me as Spence. My full name is Lewis. Lewis Spencer, named after my grandfather on my mother's side, a merchant seaman she only ever saw photographs of. No one has called me either of those two names for years, and I think there's something about the look of me that makes me feel as though I never fully earned all the syllables I was assigned. I suited something curt, something stocky that in the wrong light might be mistaken for strong. I've never really had a family to speak of, and perhaps that made me better prepared for life at the end of the world than most. I was, in my own mind, already a survivor. I was already used to looking out for myself and keeping away from the deep gravity wells of other people's trouble.

Taken as a whole, my mother and father were fleeting presences in my life. When they were together, they didn't get on; when they were apart, they pined, because they were the only ones who couldn't remember how terrible they could be. When I got older, I tried to intervene. I'd tell them to move on, find someone else, and that's when the volume would rise and the belts would come out. They didn't even care I was too big to hit any more.

Not everybody, I learned, wants to know the truth.

When I reached an age when legally I was free of them, I dropped out of my family like some people drop out of school. I checked in once in a while, searching for them online or spotting them from a safe distance. The fact they never came looking for me made me think twice about getting any closer. I saw they were still going about their usual push and pull. Together, apart, at war or preparing for battle. I didn't once feel responsible for them. We were all strangers to one another and whether or not we lived in same place or not would make no difference.

I was never ambitious, but I was practical. As a kid, I pretty much lived in the library. I read voraciously, because words on a page felt committed in a way words said out loud were not. I took work where I could find it. Manual work, actual hard work, was never something I was afraid of. I laboured on buildings sites, factories, farms, and ships. Gadflying from place to place until I found a poison worth pursuing. I learned skills on the job rather than training myself up for something better or new. Not long before the world went crazy, I was laid off from a car plant job which—in what might have been a personal record—I'd been holding down for the best part of three years. A guy from the office stood on a box in front of a crowd of us. Him in a pressed white shirt and navy tie, sweating through his seams as he confronted men and women in overalls, oil, and grease. The company was going through a restructure, we were told. They were making sure they could withstand the economic collapse their experts had foreseen.

"All bullshit," someone said in the bar afterward. "Immigrant workers are cheaper. That's what they're really doing."

This led to a heated discussion about politics and immigration and race. I bowed out to play pool.

I ended up with a dishwashing job at a pizza restaurant chain on the city fringes, and when you're my age and you're washing dishes for a living, people are likely to believe they have the measure of you. I don't know if they're wrong, I don't know if—before then—I really cared.

That's where I was when I met Macey.

This is my horror story, I suppose. But I've told it often enough I'm no longer certain where the horror of it actually lies. The whole thing feels increasingly alien to me. It's a story that someone else has already told, and I sometimes feel as though in telling it, I'm only describing the plot of a film I once saw or recounting a dream that won't go away come morning.

Macey was a good deal younger than me. She was waiting tables, ostensibly to pay her way through her master's course in creative writing at the local university.

My experience mostly being second-hand, I always assumed creative writing students must be a genteel bunch, writing about professors having affairs or about people in frocks, but Macey wasn't anything like that. She wrote awful, horrible things. Babies in blenders, old ladies in meat grinders, genocides, and sexual assaults. Her teachers, she said, were used to the more "respectable" genres I imagined, and for all their good intentions, they didn't know what to do with her. There was enough poetry in her words, she said, that they were afraid to flush away the promise of her. They liked the weapons she had forged herself; they couldn't stand the way she chose to wield them.

Macey stayed late sometimes, tapping out stories on her laptop as I finished my chores in the kitchen. Aaron, the head chef, would be out smoking joints around the back of the building with Joe, the barman, and Pinky, the sous. Aaron was a tin-pot kitchen tyrant, who measured his ego against the more malevolent chefs from reality TV. He'd come back later in the evening stinking of weed; he'd dump his knives next to the sink and then be off without a word. I didn't care. I liked having the place to myself. To ourselves. Me and Macey.

There was never anything between us, if that's what you're thinking. I never thought of her in those terms and I'm sure she never considered me as anything more than a friend or an ally, but I know where people's minds go when they hear stories like this. I told you it was a love story, but it's not one between me and Macey, so put that thought out of your head.

On nights when Macey wrote, I'd polish the surfaces, mop the floors, and scour the dishwasher. I'd haul the bags of rubbish and recycling down the network of service corridors to the bins. Sometimes while I worked, Macey read me what she was working on and my god, it would make your hair curl.

She'd shrug. "I don't know. Maybe it's a cry for help?" And her grin would be wicked and dazzling. She didn't believe any of that. She wasn't writing stories like she did because she was damaged or dark—from what I could tell, she was better adjusted than most people I knew. She found it fun. *Interesting*, she said. "People's reactions to them are the most interesting of all."

The crazy stuff was already sneaking in by then. Little cracks in the societal structure everyone stepped over with a little skip rather than stopping to figure out how to resolve.

Remember that newsreader? What was his name? Mitchell somebody. Mitchell Teale? Remember how he went apeshit on the ten o'clock news? Mid–news report, he stopped reading his autocue and went on a full-blooded Peter Finch rant about the dead coming back to life. In the old days, they'd have cut to something else, but you know how network executives were back then. All those clicks they could get from something going so gloriously off script. The security guys dragged him off camera eventually. He bounced back into the frame twice, his face puce, his eyes bulging. Then he clobbered his co-anchor, Sharon Kelly, and she disappeared under her desk like she'd folded up. Everyone thought it was pretty funny at the time, even though he was genuinely disturbed, and it was later reported how she needed stitches across her scalp. Shorn of consequences, slapstick violence always travels well. The clip went viral in the crass way things like that used to, and before anyone knew what it meant, the gleam in his eye—that glittering, fanatical keenness we would come to know so well—was visible on every television, laptop, and mobile phone. Looking outward at us all as we looked in.

Remember the clip of two men in Times Square? That was a few weeks later. Two businessmen in suits, standing on a corner, surrounded by cut-price superheroes and bright neon signage. The quality wasn't very good, but it was good enough for a debate. Some people said the men were kissing, some insisted one was biting the neck of the other. He was eating him, they said. *Eating him!* And for every person who said it was one thing, there was someone else who'd say the opposite. You could watch it side by side with a friend and you'd each see something different. It was the new gold/blue dress optical trick, the new yanny/laurel audio illusion, the new *test* to see which side of the imaginary divide you belonged.

There must have been thousands of think pieces and analyses of the Times Square clip and what it said about you depending on what you saw.

"If the only way your brain can process the sight of two men kissing is to assume cannibalism is more likely or palatable, then I don't know what to say to you."

That sort of thing.

No one ever found the two men, though, so no one could ever be really sure what the truth was. Eventually, someone did step forward, claiming to have been the "victim" in the scene, but it was bullshit and the lie was later exposed. He was an out-of-work actor, looking for notoriety to fuel his career.

More uncertainty to thicken the pot.

Me? I saw the blood. A great gout of the stuff made blocky and dark with the video's resolution. I wanted to see the love between the two of them, I really did. But when I watched it, again and again, all I saw was one terrified man and one revenant, a hollow eyed, ravenous *Other*. He lurched forward, swift as a raptor snatching prey out of the sky. I saw the blood. Every time, I saw the blood.

But I didn't tell anyone.

"They're clearly making out," I said.

Clearly.

It didn't end there. That was only the beginning. Pictures, videos, sound recordings. Remember the one of kids running through a school playground? Were they screaming? Was something chasing them all? Or was it merely the sound of kids at play? Kids running because kids like to run, or was there a look of panic on their faces as an unseen predator bore down on them from just off-frame?

Or what about the girl with the little dog? You know the one I mean. What did you see, I wonder? What did I see? You can probably guess. It wasn't pretty.

It had already started. The world was tipping, its

weight shifting, and no one had noticed how precarious the ground beneath our feet had become. Every image, every video feed, everything we heard and read seemed to have two sides. Each piece of evidence divided us, and with each line drawn, a wider slice of reality was thrown into question. The truth became slippery, as though the information itself had become a carrier. With each broadcast, the gleam in one person's eye found a home in a multitude of others. And with enough confusion, enough doubt, well . . . that's when the believers started to take charge.

Macey was a believer. She had a way of judging each moment, and you could see which way she fell by the arch of her eyebrow.

"This is such bullshit," she'd say with a conviction that instantly sold me on whatever truth she was peddling, consciously or not. She talked to me about politics in decisive terms. She took the opposite political side to my old colleagues at the factory, but her vehemence reminded me of them. She talked about television shows and comic books with the same kind of zeal. The canon of popular culture as candy-coloured gospels to be built up and torn down.

It was a Saturday when the world finally broke.

As ever, hindsight recolours the change so it felt more inevitable and less abrupt. Over the weeks before, it was true I was cloistering myself a little, although working in restaurants always puts you in a slightly different time zone, so it's a detail that probably wasn't as telling as I pretend it is. The stairwell in the building where I rented a studio flat started to stink, as though one of the residents had forgotten something in their icebox. I started leaving the window open but that only seemed to make it worse. I spent hours scrubbing the floors behind the fridge and the oven, on the off-chance I was the problem.

A smell was brewing in the restaurant as well. At the time, it felt *different*, as though my senses were sharpening enough to identify different types of rot. More noxious, like an entire carcass left out in the open somewhere.

I wasn't the only one to notice, but—my position being at the bottom of the ladder—I was the one assigned the task of rectifying it. Lorraine, the shift manager, lurked behind me as I mopped down the floors with disinfectant before and after each service, muttering about health inspectors, Trip Advisor reviews, and severance packages.

Not everyone was aware, though. That was the catch. A reasonable number of the waitstaff seemed oblivious, and very few of the customers passed comment.

On the Friday before, Aaron had some things he wanted to say.

"Whatever you smell in this kitchen, is based on my cooking," he said. "So, if you've got something to say, say it to my fucking face or shut the fuck up."

Pinky, bless her, spoke up in our defence. In a small and apologetic voice, she made the observation that there was clearly something *else* smelling somewhere; something that *detracted* from the wonderful smells of Aaron's cuisine. It was unfair to Aaron, she argued, if it should go unexplored.

Aaron stood very close to her, glowering so his face was red and glistening.

"Bull. Shit," he said.

And that was the last time we discussed the matter in his presence.

"Hypothetical question," Macey said. It was afternoon, a few hours until the dinner service would begin in earnest. "If our chef can't smell anything, how can he *taste* anything?"

"Maybe he's ill?" I said. "Congestion, perhaps?"

"Maybe . . . just maybe, he's a crap cook." She smirked. "Do you think we should ask him? I'm going to ask him."

"Macey—"

"Hey, Aaron!"

It's with some shame I admit I focussed on washing the dishes intently while the voices cranked skyward behind me.

Aaron had always had a prickly relationship with the waitstaff, something Macey got a kick out of exacerbating. It was clear the whole episode had made him feel tender and isolated, and it wasn't a complete surprise when he hammered on Lorraine's office door to demand a meeting.

Lorraine, who didn't have time for this nonsense, tersely asked Macey for an apology. Macey, who couldn't care less, refused. Lorraine gave Macey a warning and Macey gave Lorraine the finger. Lorraine would have fired Macey on the spot, but she was short-staffed for the weekend as it was.

Afterward, Macey told me the ultimatum didn't sound quite as impressive as it should have.

"I never want to see you again," Macy's impersonation of Lorraine was cruel but accurate. "After the day after tomorrow."

It was Friday night and we were sitting at the patio tables, looking out over the empty car park. I asked her if she was going to bother coming in again. She'd lit a cigarette but seemed too distracted to smoke it properly.

"Money's money," she said. "It wasn't exactly the mic drop moment I might have been hoping for, I confess."

"What are you going to do?"

She shrugged. "I don't know. Find somewhere else. Lie about why I quit this one."

"I thought you were fired?"

"I totally quit this one." She gave me a sweet smile. "Maybe you can give me a reference? They don't know what you do here. I'll get them to email you."

"Macey, come on."

"Oh, don't tell me you've never done anything slightly illegal—"

"Macey—"

"Aren't you a convict or something?"

"No! Who told you that?"

"I don't know. Only you kind of look like one. Don't look at me like that, I think it's kind of cool. You should totally lie about it. Get more tattoos."

"Dear Mr Manager, I can absolutely recommend Macey for this job. Yours sincerely, Spence, a convict."

"Alright, when you put it that way . . ."

"So, where you going to go? You could work in a bookshop—"

She nearly spat. "I'm not working in a bookshop," she said. "Every asshole in my class wants to work in a bookshop. 'It would be my dream job! I *write* books, I *sell* books.' Please. People who work in bookshops are the worst. They're . . . I dunno, capitalist librarians."

"I thought you liked books!"

"I do!" She shook her head. "But I want to write them. I don't want to have to sell someone else's books. Most people's books are shit!" She pointed the cigarette toward me. A column of ash fell to the table. "I would only open a bookshop if it didn't sell anyone else's books, just mine. It would be amazing. I'll sort out a loan on Monday."

We talked until late, and when we parted, she threw me a wave like she normally did when she left for the evening. "See you tomorrow, then," she said. "One more time."

This is what happened.

On Saturday, the restaurant was holding one of its weekend family days, fuelled by vouchers cut from flyers and magazines. At lunchtime, the tables were clogged with busy family units and their greasy offspring. The day was tense from the get-go. Macey and Aaron were avoiding one another, while Lorraine pretended nothing had happened, because it was one more thing than she wanted to deal with. Even on the restaurant floor there was a tense expectation in the air, like the endless buildup to a firework display on a cold evening. It was a long and busy shift and the dirties were stacking up fast.

I don't know exactly when matters tipped from one state to another. Perhaps it was appropriate it was Macey who told me the world had ended before I got to see it for myself.

I was alone in the kitchen. A brief lull in orders let Aaron and Pinky disappear for a secret smoke. I heard a sound from the restaurant floor, a blossom of that smell again slipping through the clouds of lemon detergent. Then Macey was in the kitchen, slamming the door behind her as best she could, her hands moving all over its seams, hunting for latches.

"Is there any way of locking this thing?" she said.

I was startled.

"How do we lock this door?" she had her hands in the air. I'd never seen her panic before. I didn't recognise the light in her eye.

"I don't think we can." It was a swing door—meant to be easy to open with both hands full, not designed to keep anything tangible out or in. Macey started shifting bins toward it, building a wall with them.

"What are you doing?"

"It's gone crazy out there."

She gestured to the serving hatch.

"They're monsters. Everywhere," she said.

"Macey, it's Family Day. They're only kids, high on sugar—"

"No, Spence, they're monsters. Literally. They're eating the customers."

I looked at her. "They're not eating the customers," I said.

"They are! Jesus Spence, what do you think that noise is? People are screaming."

And she was right, they were.

Or at least they were at that moment. As soon as she told me what I was supposed to be hearing, I heard it. The clatter and conversation of the restaurant lunch rush was immediately replaced with the worst kind of animal noises; the smell of baked pizza crust and melted cheese was substituted completely with the unmistakable smell of rotting meat. Macey spoke and the world clarified as though her description of it served as a corrective lens.

Macey remained blocking the doorway. Her voice was carefully controlled as she went through what was happening as though she was reading bullet points off an autocue.

"People are turning into monsters. The monsters are eating the people who are left. It's carnage out there. Look."

She gestured again to the serving hatch. She didn't say anything else; she didn't need to. In the weeks leading up to that day, she'd probably said enough. Neither of us knew it at the time but she'd been subconsciously laying groundwork to overthrow reality.

She had preached and I had been converted.

I looked out the serving hatch as I'd been instructed. The floor was full, but Macey was right. It wasn't full of people. They *were* monsters, all of them. Monsters that had once been people. The same hollow eyes, the same revenant greed I'd seen in the Times Square video and more like it. The scene came into focus at once; a stage hypnotist's fingers snapped in my face and the world shifted. The funny thing was, I remember it suddenly making sense. All the tension, the uncertainty, the knot in the pit of my stomach that had been there since I don't know how long. It was gone in that one moment. There was *us* and there were *monsters*. It was so simple it was almost a relief.

I edged closer, drawn to the spectacle with a greedy sort of horror. Don't get me wrong, it was a grisly tableau. Not all of the restaurant's clientele and staff had changed. There were very human screams in there too. I had to search for them but they were there—real people splayed on the floor, some moving weakly, some deathly still. They were surrounded by knots of creatures who clawed strips off them, who tore at their clothes and their skins. Shoving tattered ribbons of red matter into ragged mouths.

There were textures and shapes I had never wanted to see outside a horror movie. The floor was slick with red, smeared across the bright black and white tiles. Just this once, it wasn't pizza sauce.

When I tried questioning Macey, she shut me down.

"We don't have time for this," she said. "The world has ended. Priority one: we need to get the fuck out of here."

At the back of the kitchen, the door to the service corridor crashed open and something that had once been Aaron lumbered through, bringing with him the stink of carrion. His face had collapsed and all that was left were empty eyes and bared teeth. He roared something that was mostly vowels at us. His hands jutted in front of him like palsied claws.

I hissed in surprise. Macey sighed.

"Oh, not now," she said.

I've always thought I knew how to handle myself. Someone comes at you in a bar, you take away their advantage and give them something that'll make them think twice about trying that sort of shit again. You make all these plans. You try and account for the unexpected, but events have a way of taking you by surprise and you find yourself doing what I did: standing and staring, mouth gaping like an idiot.

Macey had no such hesitation. She rushed into action without waiting or asking for assistance. She snatched up one of the iron skillets from the drying rack and swung it in a smart arc so it struck the side of Aaron's head with a hollow *clock*. He collapsed on the floor, and I swear the expression on his ruined face still managed to register some degree of surprise.

"The larder," Macey said. "Open the larder."

"Right," I said. "Of course." In reality, I had no idea what her plans were with either Aaron or the larder. I think I thought: *She's hungry! No wonder, it takes a lot out of you, lamping a guy that size.* Either way, I was more than happy to be told what to do.

I wrestled with the handle for the walk-in and clumsily pulled it wide. Before I could say another word, Macey had started dragging Aaron inside by his feet. She moved with a strength that surprised me, bumping him around the rack shelving. Once he was clear of the doorway, she hopped over his unconscious body, taking the door off me and slamming it shut with a sharp, concussive sound.

But by punctuating one sentence so decisively, she had only made room for another one.

The impact of the door rocked the shelf unit beside it. It was stacked high with the white serving porcelain and had never been properly fixed to the wall. The jolt was all it needed to teeter forward and pitch toward us. This time, I was a bit more on the ball. I grabbed Macey by the arm and we ducked out of its way, sliding across the floor as the shelves fell and landed at an angle in front of the swinging doors. This seemed fortuitous. The deafening porcelain waterfall less so.

We froze on the spot, our faces rictus masks. Something about the tone of the restaurant shifted, I crawled

Malcolm Devlin

up the counter to glance out the hatch and was greeted by a sea of blank, rheumy eyes looking my way.

"Oh," I said. Sheepishly, I closed the serving hatch and threw the bolts to secure them. It all felt faintly absurd and apologetic. I wondered how long it would hold if pushed.

There was movement on the other side of the kitchen swing doors. The thud of a body throwing itself against the woodwork. The doors jumped open an inch or two before banging up against the fallen shelf unit. Another bang, then another. A pale hand reached through the gap, its fingers spidering as it searched for a means to remove the blockage. I stumbled back to my feet and shoved the shelf so it wedged in place behind the hose tap unit. The door shuddered and was still.

"Jesus," Macey muttered.

"Right?" I said.

Behind us, the back door clattered open again, and this time, we both yelped in surprise.

It was Pinky. Her Mickey Mouse bandana crooked across her face.

"Where's Aaron?" Her eyes were wide as moons.

"In there." Macey gestured in the direction of the walk-in larder. "What's left of him, anyway."

"Oh, thank god!" she said. "He came right at me! I thought he was going to kill me." She was clutching her right forearm, a fog of red corrupting the starched bright-ness of her chef's whites. Her voice shifted down a gear: "Is he dead?"

"He didn't look well," I said.

"What happened?" Macey jabbed her saucepan at Pinky's arm.

Pinky looked at her with a dumb expression, then raised her arm, teasing back the sleeve.

"We were out the back, there," she said. "Having a smoke, you know? And he was still going on about you, Macey. And that whole business with the smell. Anyway, he wandered off, I hung around waiting for him to come back. Started checking my phone, only it was broken somehow. And then I turn around and he's . . ."

She struggled for a word.

"A monster?" Macey said.

Pinky nodded as though it was the first time the term had occurred to her.

"Yeah, that's right," she said. "Well, you must have seen him? And he was on top of me then, and he was attacking me, and then the motherfucker bit me. Can you believe it?"

She pulled the sleeve back and showed us. Quite simply, a piece of her arm was missing, as though it had been care-fully filleted, served rare in its own sauce. There was some-thing preposterous about the excess of it, and I found myself looking from the wound to Pinky and back again, as though I could make sense of the disconnect between what Pinky told us and how she acted because of it.

"We need to get you to a hospital," I concluded.

Macey, to my surprise, shook her head.

"We'd have to get through that lot first." She nodded toward the serving hatch. "There's a first aid kit in the office."

Lorraine's office was along the service corridor, closer to the bins than she preferred. Macey made for the back door, but before she could reach it, two things happened. The lights went off with a snap and the door opened on its own, spitting Lorraine into the kitchen, wide-eyed.

"What in the world—" she started before the door to the walk-in larder banged open behind her and Aaron was back, his face a furious wound. He threw a shredded arm around Lorraine's neck and dragged her into the larder with him before she could utter another sound.

The door slammed shut behind them, leaving Macey, Pinky, and me standing, shocked stupid and staring at the spot where Lorraine had been.

"Lorraine?" Pinky said, her voice cracked and delicate.

"What happened to the power?" Macey said.

"What happened to Lorraine?"

"Give me a moment." I hunted around for Pinky's blowtorch and lit it, adjusting the flow so the flame was bright and sooty. The room filled with a thin, bluish light.

"Lorraine?" Pinky said again.

I edged toward the larder door and swung it open. The shadows retreated from the torchlight, teasing away from the flame.

Cowering at the back of the larder, two monsters stared back with hollow eyes.

I stepped back and slammed the door shut.

"She's one of them," I said.

"Figures," said Macey.

––––––––––

You know all this crap; you've heard it a thousand times before. More to the point, my memory of the whole day is up and down. Even at the time, it felt like I was watching a film with half the frames missing. Everything was happening so fast, so senselessly, I struggled to keep up.

Looking back, it's hard to determine which bits were true, which bits I believed were happening, and which bits I fabricated to connect one scene to the next.

So, keep that in mind. I don't vouch for any of this.

––––––––––

This is what happened.

The power, we figured, had been cut by Lorraine. We didn't really know what her plan had been, but the breakers she must have thrown cut the power to the sliding entrance doors, so the clientele on the restaurant floor were trapped.

Macey rigged up some temporary lights, old Christmas decorations from the box in Lorraine's office, and I wedged the larder door shut, ensuring that whatever Aaron and Lorraine had become would stay put. Pinky had gone quiet, her face white. She was pressing the bandage Macey had sourced to her wounded arm, and my first assumption was that the pain and the shock of her injury had finally hit her.

I was wrong.

"She turned into one of them," Pinky said. "He *got* her, and she turned into one of them."

"Yeah," Macey said, not really paying attention. She was running her hands over the six-burner range, a frown on her face. "Nothing we could do."

"He *got* me, as well, though," Pinky said.

Macey turned back to her, looking thoughtful.

"We don't know that," I said. I looked up to Macey. "Right, Macey? We don't know that."

Time stretched, and it was only later I understood how this was the moment that would rewrite my world. I'd already chosen to capitulate to Macey's view of what was happening but at that moment, I let her choose the rules that defined how reality was destined to work. I let her decide how far we were permitted to go. My worldview teetered until she said the word.

"Well," Macey said.

Pinky didn't want to turn into a monster. Pinky was beside herself, wailing, crying, screaming. I don't have a good idea of how long we were in there, but it felt like it was a long time and for most of it, Pinky was begging us to kill her.

————————

This is what happened.

We cut the gas lines to the range. Pinky insisted on staying behind to light the ignition. She would go up with the restaurant. Macey assured her it would be glorious, and Pinky and I agreed.

Macey and I crept through the back door, and we'd reached the edge of the car park before we stopped to look back. I saw someone at the restaurant door, banging on the buckling glass with crimson palms. A woman, her face so painfully human, so painfully alive.

"Someone's in there," I said. "A real person."

Macey shrugged. "They'll be bitten," she said. "Like Pinky. She'll turn. Nothing we can do for her now."

For a moment, I wanted to ask her how she knew. What if we weren't in the particular horror movie she clearly thought we were in? What if the rules were different now this was actually happening? I didn't know it then, but it was a final moment of clarity that might have saved me from the narrative. But I didn't say anything, I let it pass until it was forgotten. I stood with her while the restaurant fireballed at the far end of the tarmac. All that grease and oil, all that flour and salt. You should have seen it. It burned bright and beautiful like a chain that had been tethering us being cut loose and free.

We didn't wait for it to settle; we turned our backs on the inferno and fled together into the new world.

———

This is what happened.

It should have brought down the law, the army, the media, anyone. But it was only one incident of many. A single spark in a glorious firework display. No one knew where to look that day.

Eight families were in the restaurant. Parents, children, grandparents, family friends. Aside from Aaron, Lorraine, and Pinky, we killed twenty-eight customers and five further staff members, not to mention the casualties in neighbouring businesses. The fire raged until well into the night.

I know all their names. I have photographs of some of them. I keep the list folded in my wallet. They were real people. They are *my* people now, my responsibility.

Ironside helped me track them down. They have a whole department dedicated to reconciliation. A small team of researchers with clearance to trawl through the official records. The paper trails are still there if you can get behind the firewalls, although it's only something done when they think you're ready. It's an important step, they say, but it's not the most important step.

"Remember it was the infection," Awad will tell you, his own repetition, his own mantra. "It was the narrative. It's not your fault. Say that after me: it wasn't my fault. Right? You have to remember that."

There was the infection and then there was the narrative, the one holding the door open for the other. These days, we still tend to conflate them: it's easier to think of the infected, the uninfected, and the cured, but there's always been a bit more to it than that. Most of us didn't even realise there had been an infection until it was too late. A cough, a sneeze, a day in bed, and then we all moved on. Most of us didn't learn the truth until we'd been suckered in by the narrative and fallen through its wormhole.

I still don't really understand everything. My access to

information has been limited, so I have only a vague assurance of those who understand more, that it does all make sense somewhere down the line.

Awad sometimes lets things slip. For every article saying the infection was related to some kind of neurosyphilis, he says, there are a dozen which say it's very different and much more complicated. There's a fancy name for it, one of those long Latin ones that sounds like poetry, but I can never remember. All you need to know, Awad tells us, is after the minor symptoms passed, the infection hung in there, disseminating itself to the brain and the spinal column—hard to find, harder to remove—it lay dormant, waiting.

When the dominant narrative started to snowball, the infection short-circuited our reason. It drip-fed us confirmation bias. It took the lie and weaponised it.

And so, it is true to an extent that what I did wasn't my fault. We didn't know it, but we were the diseased ones and everyone we saw as an Other was not. We had the narrative—constructed over the long haul by misunderstandings, groupthink, pop-culture, and paranoia. It fed our brains the wrong signals. The infection boosted them, it stripped out everything else. God help us, it showed us what we *wanted* to see.

It was not my fault.

And yet.

Not everyone infected fell for this narrative. Some people, a lot of people as it turns out, were immune. Or smart. Or sceptical enough not to blow the world to hell. The infection remained dormant in them because they never needed to believe the bullshit everyone else was perpetuating. They never saw dead people; they never saw the world ending. They never took up a knife, a gun, a baseball bat. They never set a gas explosion that killed fourteen kids and their families.

I always come back to the commentary about that Times Square video. If you're the sort of person who sees blood and monsters rather than somebody real? What does that say about us, I wonder? What does that say about me? Does it take a certain sort of mindset to succumb to that sort of narrative? A certain sort of vulnerability to look at someone, a group of people and think: *monster, zombie, Other*.

But.

Nobody turned into a monster, nobody bit anyone else. The joke was on me, on the rest of us. If Pinky hurt her arm trying to escape what she imagined Aaron had become, then it was the infection that sold the narrative he had bitten her; it became the easier thread to process.

It was all bullshit in the end. The dead didn't come back to life. I shouldn't have to say this, but that sort of thing simply doesn't happen.

Thank god, maybe? It should come as a relief, I suppose.

But I wouldn't learn any of that until around three years later, when I was finally cured of the disease that made me see monsters, that made me believe I needed to survive them at all costs. Three years and who knows how many dead by my hands, when the gleam in my eye—so bright and vivid and *hungry* as Macey and I walked away from the burning restaurant—had finally been extinguished.

3

I shouldn't be saying this, but it's easy to escape from a place like Ironside. For all the weight of its name and its purpose, the most secure walls keeping us in are those built by the knowledge that none of us has anywhere better to go.

Yes, there are checkout procedures and recommendations. There's a whole system of halfway houses and a schedule of regular check-ins. The infection in us has been trussed up and while the narrative might come back, we're no longer contagious in the way we once were. If they suspected you were in the slightest danger of relapsing, they'd have already whisked you somewhere more secure by now. For most of us, the door is open if we choose to use it; the balmy, dusty air of Swann Road outside is ours if we do so much as ask.

I packed light. I didn't have much anyway. I stuffed some spare clothes into a carrier bag and figured it would have to do until I found something better. I had a sense, I think, that because I'd considered myself a "survivor" before, I thought I knew what I needed, but the practicalities of the world as it *really* was still confounded me. I didn't have money, I didn't have food, I didn't have weapons. Back before I was cured, I didn't go anywhere without—at the very least—a machete hanging off my belt loop. Now the idea felt both laughable and oddly empty.

I found myself standing in the door of my room, staring at the four walls as though I might be able to fold them down and bring them with me. That precious little space, with its thin partitions and its narrow cot bed. For a brief episode of my life, it had been mine and mine alone.

"Come on," Leila said. She was jostling behind me, the old army kit-bag already slung across her shoulder. I wondered if she'd been planning this excursion for longer than she'd admitted.

It was simple. We waited in the laundry doorway until the coast was clear. We took the back door. If anyone saw, no one cared enough to stop us.

―――――――

In my early days at Ironside, I was afraid of the outside. My time inside had allowed me to develop a different sort of agoraphobia. The sheer space compared with the familiar common rooms and corridors I had been navigating for the past two years; the idea I now had the freedom to go anywhere, to do anything? It was dizzying. It was like finding you could walk, having been told you'd never do so again.

Leila took it all in stride. Ironside had strait-jacketed her, and outside she was fully alive again.

It was a clear spring day, and the blunt warmth of the sun was undercut by a stiff breeze that served as a refreshing contrast to the thick stillness of the Ironside common room. The trees were dense with birds, singing discordantly at such a volume and range I wondered how I could have ever missed them. Like so much of the world, they had carried on oblivious to the way I had filtered them from my existence. Now they seemed louder, more populous, as if they finally had the space they needed to thrive.

It was the first time I had really seen the outside world since my cure. Back then, I'd been driven to the facility, bundled into a van with a handful more strays. I was still confused, still lost. The gravity of the truth had come in a rush and I didn't even know what world I was in anymore. It was difficult to orientate myself without the blanket of the narrative to make things clear to me.

Remember how you couldn't judge things like you used to? What was safe, what wasn't, what's good, what's bad? It wasn't possible to *know* by looking. Everything is so damned difficult when you have to assess it from first principles.

Leaving with Leila, it struck me there was an imperfect aspect to the outside that made it strangely, beautifully human at a level I had only recently felt qualified to understand. The world has always been bigger than us as a species, and it's only our own limited viewpoint that makes us think we'll ever be in a position to destroy it so decisively. Coming out of Ironside, I felt oddly confident that something of the natural world would endure, something would make a paradise of the shithole state our species seemed destined to leave the environment in.

The suburb where Ironside was located already bore the signs of such continuity. It had always been green and hilly, but now the remaining houses looked more precarious. The dense forest had taken over. The roads pitched up and down, and the once carefully curated streets and parks and gardens and patios were mostly quiet, their razored straight lines softened by the encroaching mosses and foliage. The jumble of white and grey rooftops crawling up the hillsides had discoloured to a subdued palette of yellows and greens. It wasn't the end of the world we had imagined; it wasn't some magical utopia either, it was simply a place where life endured. A place where the balance had shifted. People still lived here, but their status had changed. They were no longer the dominant concern.

Most of the city's uninfected population lived to the north of the river, where territory was easier to defend: the old central business district, the valley, the inner suburbs. The bridges had been demolished or blocked and the remaining population were divided into cells, separate sub-communities where it was hoped the infection could be contained if matters got out of hand.

In some ways, I don't think they needed to have worried. It was harder to fall for the narrative now the trick of it had been given away. Besides, the infected were afraid of the rest of us—particularly in large numbers—seeing us only as hordes of ravenous monsters. Together, the uninfected believed they could rely on that fear, enough to assume they had the advantage.

Remember how the infection does something to our brain chemistry? When someone is about to have a stroke, it's said they can smell burning toast. To the infected, everyone else smells like rotting meat. Does anyone else remember that? It's hard to forget, isn't it? It's little wonder most of the infected keep their distance from us *en masse*. It was one of the first things the infection gifted us with; it was one of the last things the cure took away.

Not that any of this guarantees the safety of the remaining citizenry. The infected sometimes make sorties into population centres out of desperation, looking for supplies or food. There are the odd gung-ho bands who think they will wipe out all the monsters in one act of brutality and presumably claim heroic status among their peers. Everyone has heard stories about how the infected show up to commit some sort of atrocity before retreating back to the in-between lands on the city's periphery.

The way the authorities attempt to counter this still makes me laugh more than it should. You've heard the news reports—that they leave care packages out in the more isolated suburbs? Well, they're true. I've seen them with my own eyes. The idea is to reduce the chance the infected might have cause to be brave, and the subtlety is unexpected from a government agency. They plant food and fuel and medical provisions, artfully arranged on the shelves of otherwise abandoned supermarkets and convenience stores. It's a subterfuge the narrative has a way of facilitating, and the infected seem to actually believe they've found supplies everyone else has overlooked.

When you're inside, the context is sometimes hard to piece together; even our location is hard to determine if you don't know the city. The school where the Ironside Facility was established is north of the river, further to the west than where most people live. The suburb around us is still populated, but more sparsely than the central areas. The population here are older, stubborn hangers-on, although it's clear the church on Swann

Road still manages a brisk trade each Sunday, as though the minister there can see how the end of the world might be good for business.

The city skyline is visible from the windows in Ironside's east wing. The obelisks of old commerce cutting the clouds like crooked teeth. With stories of relapses, I can't blame the uninfected for being cautious about housing us so close to them. I sometimes see that fear in Sizemore's daughter when she comes to visit. It's dressed up with a quiet amiability, but there's something forced and dutiful about the friendliness and the concern. I don't know what happened between them before Sizemore was cured; it would be rude of me to pretend I can guess.

I don't think the uninfected have anything to fear from us, but I can't blame them for wanting to be absolutely sure.

Maybe we'll all have to get used to the uncertainty. Maybe that's what frightens me. The way you can get used to anything if you've got nothing better to gravitate toward.

Many of the houses Leila and I passed were boarded up, their owners having moved closer to the central business district or the population centres to the east. This had once been one of the more affluent parts of town, and some of the larger properties had developed fortifications as their residents had dug in their heels rather than move somewhere better defended. Elsewhere, there was evidence of looting, but overall the place didn't feel abandoned, it only felt *out of season*, as though it was on pause. A setback, not a defeat; it was waiting for the right moment to restart its engines, to turn the lights back on and carry on as before.

We passed an elderly man who was working in a well-manicured front garden, walled off from the road by large, barbed-wire fences. He was wearing a paper face mask and I could see the cuffs of latex gloves hidden beneath his gardening gauntlets. He stopped to watch us struggle with the heat and the road's gradient. Leila looked to the ground. I raised a hand in a wave.

"Hey," I said.

He nodded. "Hey, yourself."

When we reached the crest of the hill, Leila turned to me furiously.

"Did you know that man?"

"No," I said.

"Then why did you talk to him?"

"To prove we weren't infected," I said. "To prove we weren't a threat."

She glowered, although I could see she saw the logic in what I'd said.

"You can't do that when we're south of the river," she

said.

"You can't not when you're north of it." I offered a smile to head off the argument.

Leila had a good sense of where we were going and I followed her, doggedly, enjoying the fresh air and the exercise. We followed the bend of the river, a two-lane highway of cracked tarmac following us. When we reached the car park for a shuttered supermarket chain, Leila wanted to jack one of the cars abandoned there. She was impatient, I guess, but I wanted to walk. Walking felt like a *cured* thing to do; stealing cars felt like something a *survivor* would want, and I really didn't want to give a shit about that sort of division anymore.

We reached the southern suburbs by nightfall. The day's journey had been hard, mostly because the heat had been unsparing and the cloud cover sparse. Getting across the river proved a minor challenge, and ultimately, I'd been forced to repress my new-found distaste of larceny and help Leila borrow a rowboat moored near one of the old pontoons. No one stopped us, and if anyone saw us, no one passed comment.

The streets here were quieter than those to the north, with no traffic at all. Many of the houses had been vandalised or had simply fallen into ruin. Our plan to steer clear of any people proved to be easy enough; there didn't seem to be anyone about to avoid.

As we neared our destination, a disparate scattering of still-working streetlights flickered into life. Intermittent patrol vehicles passed by on the roads ahead of us. They were rare and noisy, easy enough to hide from. Leila moved cautiously and I followed. She still remembered how to survive, and I think a part of me envied that of her. When we reached the empty motorway, all the big box stores that had made up much of the commercial district were shuttered and empty. We paused in the shadow of the crash barrier to take stock of our situation.

Somewhere in the distance, the timbre of the windmills on the escarpment had changed from a leisurely heartbeat to a descending blade.

"There's a park over there," Leila said. "And some woodland behind the park. They'll be camped in the woodland."

It made sense. Most of the infected didn't like to camp inside buildings. The claustrophobia of a built environment makes most of them paranoid. They share a belief that the Others congregate in built-up areas, that they don't see so many in the wild. It's true, in a sense. Part of the Compassion Directives to keep the infected and the uninfected apart.

Stories within stories, some of which happen to be true.

We were only there to observe. We weren't going to be getting too close to Val's crew, we weren't going to confront anyone. It seemed like common sense to me and now we were so far from the confines of Ironside I felt the need to mention this a few times to make absolutely sure.

"Just to observe," Leila parroted back to me after the third time, her tone petulant. "I'm not suicidal," she said. It was an assurance made with the practiced tenor of a patient who had been on suicide watch in a regulated facility for the past six months.

We backtracked to the suburbs, and when we reached Katelyn Street, we found an empty detached house we could camp in for the night. Although the back door had already been smashed in with the heel of someone's boot, a cursory inspection revealed it to be reasonably easy to secure behind us. The ground floor looked as though it had been looted, but it had been a half-hearted effort. The kitchen had been trawled through and left exposed, the flooring pooling shallow puddles fringed with black mould.

Despite such indignities, the house had clearly once been loved, and showed tell-tale signs of having been vacated with haste. It had been owned by a retired couple, their family photos still looking out from the walls of the hallway. Cable-knit cardigans and horn-rims, they judged our intrusion with the contempt it deserved. A twee pre- cision dictated each decoration decision from the wallpa- per to the picture placement to the pedantic symmetry of the antimacassars on the back of each armchair. There was something heartbreaking about its polite abandon- ment. Collateral damage to a story paced too swiftly for the owners to make sense of. Change crowbarred by a narrative sleight of hand that the house and the lives it had once contained would forever remain alien to.

We sheltered in the top rooms, keeping torch and can- dlelight away from the windows. There were two bed- rooms, a main and a spare, but now we had travelled together for the day, Leila didn't want us to split up, her old instincts slotting back into place. We found blankets and eiderdowns in the untouched linen closet. Safety in num- bers, Leila said. She didn't add that you only have to run faster than the slowest in your group. I imagined she consid- ered it.

"And I'm not sleeping on the bed," she said, regarding the neatly made double with suspicion. "I've always thought it was bad luck to sleep in dead people's beds."

"We don't know they're dead," I said. "They were probably only relocated with everyone else."

"Well, they're not happy, then," Leila said.

"I don't think it's bad luck to sleep in unhappy peo- ple's beds."

"Still."

We found spaces on the floor, beneath the line of the windows. Her at one end of the room, me at the far side. We made ourselves comfortable, but we didn't sleep.

I asked her to tell me about Val, about the people we were going to see.

She shook her head and asked me to tell her a story.

"I only know horror stories," I said. She nodded anyway.

So, I told her pretty much what I told all of you. My story, me and Macey and Aaron and Pinky. Leila had heard parts of it before, in group, but I think that was the first time I told her everything in order. I told her about the pocket full of people I still had with me. She didn't ask to see any of them and she didn't ask what happened to Macey, and I suppose I was grateful for that.

What she *didn't* do was tell me her story and although I did want to hear it, I didn't push her. A story told under duress is not the story ready to be told. Instead, she sighed and looked around the room, settling on the old CRT television propped on the dressing table and facing the empty bed.

"Do you know what I think is funny?" she said. "I remember, when I was with them, part of Val's group. When we went on supply runs deeper into the towns, sometimes, I'd go and look through the windows to see the *Others*, milling about in the houses as though nothing had happened. Did you ever do that?"

I nodded. The way she nearly spat the word *Others* made me flinch with recognition. It was strange to think how the term had spread amongst the infected, as though it were a symptom of its own.

"This was later on, you know, when we started to get a bit cocky. When *they* stopped coming to get *us*. The lull, you know? We were sneaking in closer to the built-up areas. Getting brave. I used to be fascinated by them. Val always said it was a bad idea. They're not people anymore, he'd say. Not real people. He was firm on that point. *Really* firm, you know. *They* were beyond help. But still. I'd have to look, because even then, there was something strange about seeing them. Wandering around houses as though they did still live there. As though they *were* still real people."

"They *were* real people."

"I know that now!" I wasn't sure if the anger in her voice was aimed at me or herself. "But we used to see them watching telly or looking at phones or computers. And all I could see were blank screens, snow, static, you know. Broken people poring over broken machines." Her hands were on her head, clawed, restless, as though she could snatch something away. "And I remember thinking to myself, look at these poor fools. They're still going about what they think of as normal life. They're still acting out impulses to consume, consume, consume. Staring at blank televisions, pawing away at phones and laptops like they actually mean something.

"Aren't I lucky, I would think. I really would actually think that: *Aren't I lucky*, I broke free of all that sort of shit. Back to nature, back down to earth, fighting for my life. So much more *alive* than any of these sad fuckers."

She deflated a bit and shot me a wry expression.

"But no, they really were all just watching TV and chatting with mates or whatever. And I was off living in a ditch, stinking like shit and actually feeling smug about it."

She shook her head.

"Fucking nuts," she said.

I took a breath.

"You going to tell me about Val?" I said. "About what we're walking into tomorrow?"

"Just observing," Leila said. "I promise."

"Still."

She sighed, burying her head in her arm. When she glanced up again, she looked tired.

"Not now," she said. "I'm sorry, I can't."

"It's okay."

"Tomorrow, then?"

"Okay."

Instead, we talked about the politics we had both missed and which neither of us fully understood. The country was still running, for the most part, but it was struggling, everyone was. A lot of people got infected and no one group was above falling under the spell of the narrative's cheap twists and turns. Certainly not politicians, certainly not the military. What we did know was that infrastructure had fractured in the most bizarre ways and held firm in stranger ones. Leaders had been deposed by their secretaries; whole units of the armed forces went rogue, while various factions struggled to keep them in check. It must have been madness, but both Leila and I, trapped in our Rip Van Winkle apocalypse dreams, missed it all.

Since then, we'd both had only breadcrumbs. The news had mostly been kept from us, the truth rationed, so we only understood what we could witness for ourselves.

This is what we assumed: While real governments saw the rise of the Others with the rest of us, shadow governments were set up to temper and redirect them. Things were bad early on, we learned. Governments in various parts of the world with their itchy fingers and weapons of mass destruction? It was a miracle, we agreed, there was a world to wake up into.

We talked about the Compassion Directives and tried

to make sense of them. In one respect, they sounded too good to be true, but I couldn't get my head around the fact they were so cynically named. True compassion is never a last resort, wheeled out when all remaining possibilities have failed. We didn't need to have been watching the news since our cure to appreciate the directives had come late in the game, after countless changes of administration. First came violence, then coercion. The usual peacocking displays of power. Strong-arm tactics, strongly worded disapproval.

None of which worked against the narrative, they only fed it and made it fat.

Sending the army in exacerbated the infection. It reinforced the division for those already afflicted and worse, it spread the narrative among those sent to repress it. The sheer fervour of the infected they had been ordered to put down served as a recruitment drive. You can't target fanaticism with a firefight, and the narrative was contagious in a way the military had no way to protect themselves against. Before long, the gleam was visible on both sides: flickering in the eyes of the army boys with their giant guns, seeing their compatriots slavering and hungry around them . . .

Well, you can imagine what happened. Who, after all, is more susceptible to survivalist fantasies than those armed and primed to enact them?

Both Leila and I had experience of the opposite side, seeing the army rushing toward us as a horde of furious revenants blocking every exit.

Macey died during one such siege.

Or at least that's how I've always told the story.

4

This is what happened.

The Others were laying siege to the Five and Bean Cafe on the corner of Lewis Avenue.

Inside, there were nearly a dozen of us. Stragglers, orphans, and refugees Macy and I had picked up along the road. It felt like a lifetime had passed since we'd torched the restaurant, and now it was Macey who burned brighter than ever. Drawing survivors like a beacon flame.

We had been in the process of moving to a newer, bigger camp, and our expedition had ventured too close to the river in search of supplies. It was early days, and the rules of the game were still hazy pencil lines in a margin rather than letters carved into stone.

We'd met back at the cafe, having split into parties to raid the remaining shops in the area. One of our groups had been spotted on their way back to the rendezvous and now the street outside was heaving with a sea of angry, dead people. There was a roar of shredded lungs and the stench of rotting meat. Above it all, the temperature had risen to a thick humidity that made the cafe feel less like a sanctuary and more like a pressure cooker, which threatened to kill us all, even if we outlasted the revenants outside.

The survivors looked to us: to Macey for her leadership, to me because I had been following her longest. People were restless, afraid, but the only whiff of mutiny I sensed was from Jeff Cotter, a businessman in shirtsleeves who was muttering something about leadership, morale, and team building.

Macey, bless her, was in her element. She started barking orders on cue: Barricade the back doors, protect the windows, search for alternate exits. Upstairs was a flat we'd already broken into. I'd done some contracting work in this part of town some years earlier and I remembered the narrow attic spaces across the block of units were joined. A short cut masked with flimsy partition walls, that a bit of judicious kicking would take care of. With enough brute force, we could open up a passageway and make our way along the street unseen, escaping down the fire escape at the western end.

"Good," said Macey. "But if you're all going to be making noise up there, we need to keep their attention here."

"I can do that," I said.

She shook her head. "Spence," she said. "It's sweet you might think that you could ever be louder than I am." She kissed me on the cheek. "Go kick some walls down."

And that's what we did. Macey started singing the Marseillaise at the top of her lungs and I led a demolition crew upstairs. We had cleared a path through three of the units by the time the shooting started. Macey's group had started picking off the Others from the upstairs window, and the noise and the smell of blackened blood got the crowd of revenants all riled up into a frenzy.

"Keep going," I told my crew, and I retreated back to the cafe to the sound of glass breaking, bodies throwing themselves through the windows. I arrived to chaos. Little Susie Quina was too close to the windows. They shattered behind her, and long-fingered hands swiped at her blue greatcoat. She toppled backward, where a waiting claw swung at her like a sickle, taking out her throat in a brisk red mist. Jeff Cotter was grabbed by his feet and dragged through the broken window, shredding into pinstriped streamers as he went.

Macey was surrounded, her ammunition spent. She was still singing although it now sounded mostly like a roar. I remember her waving a pair of kitchen knives around her in a whirl of glinting steel. She was slicing the Others left and right but there were far too many of them, even for her. Seeing her on the verge like that, my blood boiled.

"Retreat!" I yelled. "Up the stairs. Now."

Survivors pressed past me as I fought my way to Macey and dragged her up the stairs. We barricaded the door, which gave us a little time. We heard the signal from the end of the block. The last wall had been breached. The route was clear. I held her in my arms as our companions ran past us.

Macey was bitten. Macey was bitten badly. Macey was dying. But the gleam in her eye? It burned so bright we both knew it would survive us all.

"Well," she said. "This . . . this sucks."

I agreed. I always agreed.

"We'll patch you up," I said. "See what we can do. Have you back on your feet again, right as rain."

"No," she said. "Don't be an idiot. You know exactly what you've got to do."

"I'm not going to leave you here."

"Damn right you're not," she said. "You're going kill me. You're going to take that sawn-off shotgun and you're going to redecorate in here."

"Macey."

"*Spencer*. Spence. You're going to kill me because although you look like a fucking hobo, you're a gentleman who is absolutely not going to let me become one of those assholes."

She coughed, and for a moment it sounded so theatrical I wondered if she was having me on. But she was pale

and bleeding. Her wounds too deep and real to be anything less than serious.

"For fuck's sake, Spence." She laughed, a tiny little
laugh. "Don't make me eat you, you dumb motherfucker.
I mean, when was the last time you bathed? You'll taste
awful. You'll give me food poisoning. It'll be *so* embar-
rassing."

"Fuck you."

"No. Fuck *you.*"

I held her for a long time. I never had the words back
then to say what I wanted to say.

A handful of people were hovering around us, trying
to figure out if they could run or help or strengthen the
barricades on the door.

"Get the fuck out of here," I said to them.

"Lead the way," Macey said.

————————

It didn't occur to me then, that my version of the story
was no more or less true than different accounts I would
hear later.

Enough time had passed for Macey to have become
known as a leader, even by those who never met her.
When she died, she slipped so easily into legend. Perhaps
it was seeing how this branch of the narrative grew and

divided and divided again that made me see how the truth had become so malleable.

I remember hearing the same story told around a different campfire. I was hidden in the shadows of the group, ignored, anonymous. I barely reacted when my own name came up in less than flattering terms.

This is what they said happened.

The Others were laying siege to the Five and Bean Cafe on the corner of Lewis Avenue. They'd seen Spence as he raided the nearby houses and followed him back to the meeting place. Now the streets were full of the ravenous undead.

Macey took command, because Macey always knew what to do. She stood on a table like a general about to inspect her troops. Like a fucking badass, she unsheathed her looted samurai sword.

"The attics in this building are all joined," she cried out. "We can escape that way. But someone needs to stay behind to hold them off."

She turned to Spence, who gawped at her with puppy eyes. He was older, he had always been weak. Everyone knew she could do better. Everyone knew he was holding her back.

"Stay with me, Spence."

The old fool shook his head. "I gotta get out of here," he said. Probably to piss himself. He ran away.

Macey held her ground. There were tears in her eyes. Macey started singing Les Mis. We all joined in. It was so fucking beautiful. The Others came through the windows. Glass shattered, blood sang. Macey swung her blade in arabesques. The creatures' blood sprayed the coffee tables around us.

But there were too many of them. They kept coming. Our numbers dwindled; Macey was surrounded.

"Go!" she shouted at the rest of us. "Save yourselves, my friends!"

"We want to help!" we said. Bodies hit the floor. We could all still hear music.

"No!" Macey cried. "Follow Spence. He needs you now."

Our fury fuelled us.

"Spence is a coward, let us help you!"

"Go!"

We tried to help but she was overwhelmed. The Others came in a tide. Together they tore her apart.

But she gave us the time to escape.

Alone, she held them off for long enough to save us all.

It was the army that killed Macey, not the Others.

Awad argues that we should try and identify all perspectives. "Events happen in more than two dimensions," he says. "You have to imagine how they look from different sides, otherwise you don't see them at all."

He's right, but I still react first and have to check myself. For a while I thought I should hate the commanders who gave the order to open fire, but they acted as they used to act, before the Compassion Directives redirected them. They were living people. They had a story of their own.

———————

This might be what happened.

The army arrived on Lewis Avenue after reports were received that a sizeable group of infected had been seen in the area. They had already looted local businesses and killed six people who had defied the curfew, remaining in their property to defend what they still saw as their livelihoods.

The infected had gathered at the Five and Bean Cafe on the corner of the street and before long were completely surrounded by men and women in army fatigues.

Lieutenant Pivott took to the bullhorn with a series of terse demands.

He turned to Brewster beside him, binoculars clamped to his face. "What's going on there?" Pivott said.

Brewster shrugged. "Some girl's standing on a table. The rest of them are staring at her and drooling."

"Did they hear what I said?"

"I don't think they care, sir."

"Christ." Pivott hefted the bullhorn again. "They're like kids. They don't listen."

Pivott didn't have kids of his own. A few years earlier, he'd been on security detail when a foreign dignitary with a dubious human rights record had been visiting the local university to pick up an honorary degree. The students had been demonstrating. It was too quaint for a riot, but they'd kept him on his toes. They had ignored everything he had said as well. At least they hadn't been armed.

From downstairs someone had started singing. It sounded foreign, which explained nearly *everything*.

"What's happening now?" Pivott said.

"Some of them are going upstairs—"

Some of them appeared in the upstairs windows. Breaking the glass and firing.

"Jesus fucking Christ."

Pivott gave the order; the army moved in. They had training while the infected didn't. They could aim, organise. They were better equipped.

Pivott saw a woman in a blue jacket fold over suddenly. He saw a man in shirtsleeves dance in a mist of red. He saw the girl on the table get a few lucky hits, then a stocky bloke with a beard turned up to drag her away. She was kicking and screaming like she was possessed.

He turned to Brewster.

"Follow them. I mean it. Wipe the bastards out."

Brewster was staring into his face, his hand poised over his sidearm.

"Brewster?" Pivott said.

Brewster didn't reply. There was something in the man's eye that Pivott didn't like at all.

———

This is what happened.

Expediency saved us. Luck or cowardice, something like that. The narrative reshaped our experience, fed off our confusion. It sunk into us, deeper and meaner.

———

For the authorities, the solution must have come from an unexpected source. The problem was narrative. A narrative needs drama; drama needs conflict. QED. Cut off one and the other struggles to sustain itself. It becomes banal. It no longer satisfies and therefore, it withers enough for the doubters to see the holes in the story. It gives them the opportunity to be snatched away and shown the truth of the world.

I have this image of the government in a state of desperation, calling in novelists and playwrights and creative writing professors. Sitting them down in a room and hanging off their every word.

Macey would have got a kick out of that. I don't know if it's actually how it happened—it's unlikely, let's be honest—but the outcome was mostly the same. The army were ordered to stand down, to retreat and observe. Do you think they were trained up on narrative structure? The finer use of language? Imagine that: Two, Four, Six, Eight, this is how we punctuate.

Please God, may that be what happened.

Whatever they came up with, this was where the Compassion Directives came in.

Step one: Keep the infected and the uninfected apart.

Step two: Control the narrative. For the uninfected this meant the surviving media was carefully scripted, the internet ruthlessly filtered. Information could no longer be trusted and thus it was subject to the strictest kinds of quarantine. Despite all this, news about the infected was reported not with fear or hysteria, but with pity and sympathy.

It's not their fault.

Look at both sides.

And obviously, *keep your distance. For their safety and yours.*

Step three: Weaken the narrative. Make it a poorer story, make its followers *doubt* by feeding them something more convincing.

There are two types of victim infected by the narrative. The believers and the followers. The believers are the ones invested in furthering the story. They're the Maceys and Vals of the world who go all-in. They're charismatic, confident. They're the carriers of the lie, and the gleam burns so bright in them it draws the rest of us, reigniting the light in our own eyes until we see nothing other than the perspective they shape for us. The believers are the ones who can *explain* what's happening. They justify it and we simply shovel down all the shit we were fed as though it's good for us.

We are . . . or rather, we *were* dependent on them, but even when we were doggedly following them, our faith was weaker than you might expect. We needed constant reinforcement, constant fixes. Otherwise, our eyes would wander, searching for a better high.

All the cured I've ever met at Ironside are followers.

Show of hands. Who here would class yourself as a follower? Right. And a believer? Put your hand down, Sizemore, no one believes a fucking word you say. Yeah, I know. Love you too, mate, but I've got the floor so back off.

The way I see it? The trick to curing us of the narrative was to break our faith. To weaken the hold the believers had on us; to give us room to doubt and see the truth as a better story.

There was a bit of this going on in the news before the infection kicked off. The consensus at the time was, given "normal" circumstances—such as they were—muddying a political argument is more likely to strengthen faith in it.

For followers of the narrative, this wasn't entirely true. The narrative was sensationalist, already absurd. We followers wanted to believe it unconditionally, but it was occasionally a challenging pill to swallow. It was a story where the dead came back to life, for Christ's sake, where corpses staggered around and ate the living! It takes a certain mindset to accept such circumstances as normal without question.

I don't know exactly how long I'd been doubting by the time I saw.

The story had become a familiar one by then. I'd fallen in with another gang of survivors, and given the way the lull made us restless, our time was spent with the usual bickering and power games. I was mostly grateful my semi-official position as Macey's second-in-command was over and done with. Having said that, I still missed Macey. I missed her confidence, her humour, I missed the way she didn't take any shit, from either the Others or from "real" people.

Patsy and Tom were our new believers. They were young and in love, and in a perverse way their co-dependency reminded me of my parents; as if they'd stayed youthful, while I had motored on past them into late middle age. Patsy and Tom couldn't keep their hands off one another, convinced their love was only possible because of the freedom the end of the world had allowed. I sound cynical about them because I was old with grey in my beard and they were young enough that the world which had been turned upside down was one they'd barely lived in long enough to appreciate was gone.

Still, they *believed*. In all of it. The Others, the end times, the darkest things a survivor must do in order to prevail. I don't blame them for that. They were infected like the rest of us were, but I don't think I ever entirely believed in them. We were disconnected from the start; my narrative and theirs simply didn't quite click together at a human level.

I followed them anyway. It's what I did back then. We believed we were better off in groups than alone, but you could sense the tide starting to turn. Although I wouldn't have admitted it out loud, I had my eye on different groups, different ways to get by. Somewhere a bit quieter, a bit easier, somewhere less histrionic.

What we called the lull had been going on for nearly six months by then and there was this low-level hum that we might be capable of surviving alone or in smaller groups. The believers weren't having any of it, of course, and maybe that was a sign they were losing some of the power they'd once had.

Still. There was a feeling the worst was over and in truth I was glad, because I was getting tired of it all.

It was the raid that pushed me over the edge. That raid we went on to Hannigan Street, which shifted my status from agnostic to atheist. We still called them raids back then, but they were no such thing. They were looting expeditions, where we would kit up and venture into built-up areas to scavenge through the houses and shops for food and supplies. It didn't occur to us that people were restocking them to keep us contained. That sort of thinking didn't fit with the narrative, so it was easy to overlook.

On our travels, we would see the Others once in a while but for the most part they were in ones or twos, lurking in open spaces, easy to avoid. They would ignore us, and I was happy to ignore them. This raised some consternation with some in the group who thought I was going soft.

"The only good Other is a dead Other," was Gaspin's mantra.

I shut him down. It was a waste of time, a waste of ammo. Gaspin was tall, somewhere between a biker and a surfer. He had a lanky frame but it was clear he'd spent time working it, so it had thickened in a slightly preposterous way. He was the sort of man who was itching for a fight, but I couldn't be bothered anymore. The Others and I had each lost our appetite for the fight.

I found myself volunteering for the raids a lot in those days. It got me away from the soap-operatics of the camp, and for all my doubts about putting a slug through a monster's brain, there was still the promise there might be a familiar flush of adrenaline somewhere to reignite my interest in the whole situation.

On that particular day, four of us went. There was Gaspin—of course—and there was Big Bran and Kitty-with-a-Y. The outer suburbs were mostly picked clean, so we travelled inward and eastward to the corner of Hannigan Street and Barrett Road, where a convenience store had proved fruitful in the past.

It turned up trumps again on that occasion. A new stash we'd *somehow* missed before. Gaspin spotted a hatch hanging open in the stock room ceiling, and in the crawl space we found a cardboard box full of tinned vegetables, soup, and protein bars. We divvied it up, stashed it away in our bags, and regrouped on the street outside. It was still early. I wasn't in the mood to go back straight away. Patsy was always interested in debriefing when we got back, but I was happy to put that off as long as possible.

I suggested we check out some of the nearby houses. Find some more supplies.

Bran pushed back a bit. Thought it was too risky. He'd always been a bit of a coward when it came down to it. I overruled him easily enough. It turns out that when practical details are at hand, I can pass as a believer well enough to get some to follow me for the short term.

We went to three houses that day and we did alright. We found stashes of bandages and disinfectant in the first one and a whole crate of sanitary towels and pain killers in the second.

It was in the third house we found the pink room. Or rather, I found the pink room. It was the fact nobody else saw it that sent me scrambling.

We broke into the house as we'd done with the previous ones, and we split into pairs, each taking a floor to search, checking any hiding places for Others that might leap out when we weren't looking.

Kitty and I were on the ground floor, and when we opened the door to the lounge, I saw immediately the room had been painted pink, because it was a bright sunny day and the light came through the window in stripes and made the whole place glow.

It wasn't only the walls. Everything in the room was pink. The wallpaper, the ceiling, every inch of the floor. Every piece of furniture had been painted too—or re-upholstered so it all matched. All the pictures on the wall were the same blank shade, all the frames, all the ornaments on the mantlepiece, all the books in the shelves were painted the same colour. Everything was exactly the same clean, bright hot pink.

The uniform strangeness of it made me stall, but Kitty walked straight through as though nothing was amiss, as though she fully expected each of the houses on the street to have a room like it. She only stopped to look back when she realised I wasn't with her anymore.

"What's got into you?" she said when she saw the look on my face.

I struggled. "It's quite . . ." I said. "Don't you think it's odd?"

"What's odd?" She looked about her. "It's abandoned. They're all abandoned. That's not weird anymore, re-member."

And she went off to the kitchen to explore further.

I let her go. I still don't know if she was unable to regis-ter how peculiar it was, or if she simply didn't see it. The narrative had focussed her to such an extent she only saw what it needed her to see to sustain itself.

I dropped my bag on the floor and sat down in the

armchair. There was a floor-length mirror on the wall directly in front of it, the frame as pink as everything else, but the glass was clear, and in it, I caught sight of myself in the tableau. There was me looking absurdly grizzled. My beard was mostly white, my face was wind-burned and red, my clothes were torn and dirty. My machete was resting neatly across my knees and the look in my eyes was *wild*. Around me was nothing but pink.

It was a record-scratch moment, right there. The juxtaposition *grated* and somewhere in my brain, something skipped.

When Bran and Gaspin came in, they found me still sitting there.

"You tired, old man," Gaspin said. "Take a seat why don't you, while the rest of us get work done."

"Poor fella," Bran said. "Not long for the glue factory."

None of them commented on the room. Like Kitty, none of them seemed to see anything wrong with it. This wasn't an important scene in the stories they had been allotted. They'd searched the house out of diligence and found little interesting or useful to report.

"We going home?" Kitty said.

"Sure," I said. It didn't seem worth forcing the issue. Not then.

I would learn later that the pink room was one of many around the town. Random acts of grand surrealism designed to make people question what they saw. Later I would hear of different tableaus left for people to find. In one house, all the furniture in the lounge had been bolted upside down to the ceiling: a perfect replica of a middle-class drawing room, hung upside down. In another, all the dining room furniture was stacked in an impossible sculpture in the main room, bursting through a hole in the ceiling and continuing up through the bedroom. Elsewhere, a whole room was filled with red balloons. There were more pink rooms, and orange ones and blue ones. One bathroom had been reconstructed entirely at a thirty-degree angle, so the water in the sinks veered to the side in apparent defiance of gravity.

These were part of the Compassion Directives. If you noticed them, the thinking went, then it was the beginning. Because if you noticed that, then you might start looking closer at more things.

It worked on me, certainly. After the pink room, I really did start looking more intently at the details of the world around me. We were camped out of town in the warehouse district and there was a billboard across the road that had been there since I'd first arrived. I had always assumed it was an advert for a solicitors' firm. It was only after the visit to the pink room that I realised what the caption said.

THIS ISN'T REAL, it said in large letters, next to a photograph of a smiling man in a suit. Now, why hadn't I noticed that before? I thought.

It wasn't the only sign that came into focus. Once I'd seen one, more started jumping out like images from a pop-up book. While I was out on another raid, I saw dozens of the things. WAKE UP, IT'S NOT THE END OF THE WORLD, NO OTHERS. NO MONSTERS. Not only advertising hoardings on bus stops and billboards, but actual road signs and street furniture. Number plates on abandoned cars read W4K3 UP, messages written on the tarmac where road-crossings should be read LOOKS NORMAL. It was absurd, it was *funny*. It felt as though the whole world was shouting at me and only me, because none of the rest of the crew saw a damn thing.

Looking even closer, I would find more specific messages. Weather-beaten fly-posters pinned on lampposts weren't for lost children or missing pets. Cards in shop windows weren't advertising second-hand washing machines. The copy written on the back of cereal boxes had nothing to do with breakfast nutrition. They were, for the most part, directions out of the maze, but even they seemed improbable the first time I saw them. An address in the outer suburbs, not so far from Hannigan Road. Near the old bingo hall, across the road from the substation. Look for the red van, they said. Stand at the corner of the road, tap your heels together, and say: "I want to wake up."

Now I'd started seeing these messages, it became clear to me my time in the group was on notice. I was isolating myself, and that was attracting the sort of attention I didn't want. I could see they were talking about me in low voices, and I knew damned well what that meant.

"You didn't get yourself infected out there, did you?" Gaspin said. Bless him and his lack of subtlety. I wondered if he was really that stupid or if he was sweetly trying to tip me off.

I shook my head.

"Only you're acting all kind of distracted, you know?" He gave me a pointed look. "You do know what that means, don't you?"

"I'm fine, Gaspin."

He scowled.

"It's not you I'm worried about. If you're sick? If you die? I don't give a shit. Good riddance. I'm worried you could fuck up someone I *do* care about."

He ambled back to the fire without giving me another look.

I don't know how it would have worked. If I had become cured, would they have seen me as a monster straight away? Or would there have been a transition where, for a while, I was both? I don't know and I didn't stick around to find out. I left that night. I thought, *fuck it* and got the hell out of there. If they really were keeping an eye on me, no one followed, and for a brief time, I let myself come to terms with the fact I was alone, until it felt comfortable and right.

I found the bingo hall and the substation on the map and made my way there at a pace, hiding in scrubland when I thought I heard movement in the streets ahead.

The sun was coming up as I arrived. Parked on the corner, I saw a red van. An innocuous thing with a smashed-in windshield and a flat tyre. I wondered how often I'd passed it before.

So, I stood on the corner opposite and I watched it. I must have stayed there for a few hours before I summoned the courage to speak up.

"I want to wake up," I said, clear enough to be heard all the way down the road.

There was a pause, then there was a crackle, then a voice on a loudspeaker said.

"Aren't you supposed to do something else first?"

"I'm not clicking my heels together," I said. "I've got sciatica. Click-fuckity-click, take me home, Toto. How's that?"

There was another pause.

A door opened in the bingo hall across the road. A man was standing there, looking down at me from the top of the steps. He was dressed in military gear, one hand hidden behind his back.

"What you see?" the man said.

"I see an asshole hiding a handgun up his crack," I said.

He smiled. "Human or Other?"

I shook my head.

"I'm talking to you, aren't I?" I said.

There was a long pause.

"Look, man," I said. "I just want to wake up."

He nodded.

"Don't we all," he said.

5

Leila was bundled up in a blanket, leaning against the wall, but she wasn't sleeping. She was looking out the window, her expression far away. It was too dark to see if she had been crying, and I wasn't going to ask. I was reminded of the time before we first spoke, seeing her sitting in the canteen, staring out the window while everyone speculated about what she was looking at.

After so many nights sleeping in the room next door to her, it was the first time I imagined I understood the nature of her silence properly.

It wasn't so much a personal silence. It was an external stillness that served to balance an internal cacophony. It was a hyperawareness, a heightened alertness. I saw how knotted-up she was, how much the struggle to maintain her own personal order cost her. I wondered if her secret was simply that she never slept at all.

I didn't say anything because I knew it wouldn't help. I remained alert for her so she wasn't alone. I stayed awake, silent in my own way, waiting with her for the morning.

Macey once told me the worst way a story can end is by someone waking up and realising everything that happened was only a dream.

"It's a cop-out," she said. "All that carefully constructed world building, all those people who you believe in and then . . . nah, it's a lie and none of it really matters. No one wants that. We read stories, watch shows on TV, and we appreciate they're fiction. But when they come out and outright admit it, it pisses us off."

We were the last ones up around the fire. We'd been camping in the forest park for the past couple of weeks. Moving from clearing to clearing every few days, setting up patrols to watch for Others in the area. There must have been ten of us by then, our group snowballing as it bounced from one short-term sanctuary to the next.

Many had come to us in ones or twos, strangers lost in the ruins they saw of the world; drawn to the same fire of Macey's belief that had also drawn me. Even when we met different groups with their own leaders, people would peel off to join us as though her force of personality was strong enough to unseat them, send them reeling. I had known her since before the infection, but I wondered if it was something she'd always had about her. She had only needed the right time to be taken seriously, the right kind of chaos to allow her to rise gloriously to the top.

"When I was little," Macey said, "I sometimes used to have this dream. I'd have it a lot, back then. In it, I would see my mum sitting on the end of my bed. She wasn't watching me sleep, she was simply sitting there, completely relaxed, her head turned away from me. I would see the shape of her in the dark—you know that quality of darkness you get when your eyes have adjusted and everything is slightly silver, slightly grey? That's what she was. This silver figure on the end of my bed, just . . . being there. Waiting for me to wake up.

"Only, of course, I didn't want to wake up, then, because when I woke up, I knew she wouldn't be there anymore." She glanced up at me. "She died when I was eight," she said. "A motorbike accident, which makes it sound kind of cool, and I like to think she was, but she was reckless too. I get that.

"Anyway, I used to dream she was there, at the end of the bed. And I didn't want to wake up again because . . . I liked how it felt, that warm kind of dream, you know? There was something so reassuring about it."

She drew a long breath and released it expansively.

"If I were writing it into a story," she said, "I'd probably have her singing something, or I'd try and make it creepy, or I wouldn't include it at all because people fucking *hate* dream sequences in stories, but . . ."

She sighed. "It's only that I don't trust dreams. I don't think it's fair they don't really mean anything."

A movement from beyond the tree line sent my hand reaching for the machete. A figure breached the darkness and moved toward us, its pace too even and measured to be mistaken for an Other. Macey nodded in acknowledgement as it edged into the light offered by the fire.

"Gaspin," she said.

Gaspin was dressed in army fatigues and a hunting jacket. He had a machine gun cradled in his arms as though it was a child.

"Ma'am," Gaspin said.

"See anything out there?" Macey said.

"All quiet, ma'am."

Macey nodded. "Well," she said. "As you were."

Gaspin slinked off back into the trees. I swear his heels clicked together as he did so.

"Ma'am?" I said when he was gone.

"Don't tease him," Macey said. "He's heavily armed."

"I have questions about that as well," I said. "Where did he *get* something like that? Big Bran as well, have you seen the shit he's carrying around with him?"

Macey shrugged. "It's strange, isn't it?" she said. "That

people like him and Bran should have been... I don't know, *right*, I suppose."

"Right?"

"Well, not in terms of politics obviously. I mean the *end times*." She made scare quotes with her fingers. "Maybe it really was worth tooling up with weapons, stockpiling canned goods and fuel. Do you ever think it's odd that so many who didn't get infected had guns stashed in their homes somewhere? I mean, I don't for a minute believe they ever thought *this* is how things were going to end, but..."

I grinned at her across the fire. "Did you?"

She put on a show of looking affronted. "Well, no, of course not," she said.

"Only I've read some of your stories and—"

"Oh, *fuck off*." She threw a twisted dried stick at me. It missed and bounced into the undergrowth, hitting something with a clacking sound. "I've never written a zombie story before in my life. Never going to happen."

"Yeah, but... babies in blenders—"

"Babies in...? That was metaphorical, you dipshit."

"Right, but—"

"But nothing." Her voice dropped to a low whisper. "God, you think because I write horror stories sometimes that I'm on the same level as those assholes?"

"Who'd have thought you horror writers would be so

right?" I said.

"Fuck right off."

"Right-o."

_____

When I woke in the house on Katelyn Street, it didn't occur to me I hadn't intended to sleep. My first thought was that I must have slept through until the morning for the first time in years. I was alone in the bedroom, and tangled up in the remaining sleep as I probably was, I considered that perhaps Leila had never been there with me in the first place. I felt I was alone in an unfamiliar house; I felt exposed but strangely at peace. If Leila had never been there, then maybe I had never met her. Maybe I had never been cured, maybe there'd never even been a cure.

In a brief moment of disorientation and uncanny wonderment, the possibilities of objective reality danced before me, daring me to choose between them.

I don't know if it's my age, but sometimes it takes a moment for threads to come together come morning.

When I stumbled downstairs, I heard movement in the kitchen. Leila was there. Of course she was. She was trying to find the means to make coffee.

"They have instant," she said, "but the water's off. I went down the street to fill the kettle."

"Power's back on?"

"No, but the gas is. They're on bottles."

I stood in the doorway and watched her move about the room. She must have raided more than water from neighbouring houses. She was dressed in new-looking jeans, a woollen fleece, and fingerless gloves. She searched through the cupboards for something to make the coffee in.

"It'll have to be black."

"Black is fine. Did I ever tell you about the pink room?" I said.

She shot me a glance then returned to the pan on the stove. "No," she said. "I don't think so."

"It was . . ." I glanced behind me to the lounge. In the morning light it looked prim and ordered and determinedly normal. "I don't know. It was strange. How did you get cured?"

She raised an eyebrow. "How did I get cured?" she said.

"Yeah, I mean. What made you . . . you know?"

She shrugged.

"I don't know." She looked away from me, watching the pan. "Do you think we *are* cured? I don't feel cured, Spence. They say the infection doesn't go anywhere. When you've got it, you've got it. Just because we're not seeing dead people anymore, doesn't mean we're alright."

She looked at me directly. "Do you feel cured?"

It would be dishonest to pretend the question didn't throw me, but I nodded anyway. "Yes," I said. "I think so." I mock flexed my arm muscles to demonstrate. "Fighting fit," I said. "Yes."

Her smile was arch. The water bubbled. She hoisted the pan off the stove and poured it messily into the two waiting mugs.

"You talk in your sleep," she said, setting the pan back down on an empty hob. "Did you know that?"

"A lot of people talk in their sleep," I said. "What did I say?"

"Oh. Mostly nonsense." She looked away again, looking past me into the lounge, examining the paisley sprawl across the walls. When she spoke again, it was clear she was choosing her words with absolute care. "But the way you speak. When you're asleep," she said. "You don't sound cured."

She gave me a mug of coffee—instant, watery, a yellow halo creeping up the edges of the white porcelain. She edged past me with a thin smile and took the largest armchair in the middle of the room. I saw her grasp the armrests with clawed fingers and push herself back so that a footrest popped out from the base.

"I am cured." I didn't like how insistent I sounded, so I said it again, quieter, weaker.

"Cured is relative," Leila said. "Infected is relative."

"That's not what Doctor Awad says—"

"Awad is relative."

"Leila—"

"I'm not saying he's wrong," Leila said. "I'm not saying any of them are wrong. They're right. We do have to look at all sides. Compassion, yes? It's their . . . schtick. But that's what I'm saying. It's okay not to be fully cured. It's okay that things aren't exactly as they were. It's okay that . . ."

She flailed.

"Have you ever read a book," she said, "that you liked so much you read it more than once?"

"I've read lots of books." I didn't mean to sound so defensive.

She smiled. "That's not what I'm asking. I'm talking about *comfort* reads. Have you ever had those?"

I considered it, then shook my head.

"There's . . . not enough time," I said. "There's so much else to read. So many new things." I checked myself. "Well, there used to be. You know. I assume there's more out there—"

"Right," she said. "And that's fair. But sometimes, there are books I re-read. That I'm drawn back to. You can never re-read a book for the first time, and it's never really the same reading it when you know what will happen.

But . . . sometimes that's what you want, isn't it? Certainty. There's comfort in that kind of familiarity."

She lapsed into silence again and it was ungracious of me to break it.

"Is that why we're here?" I said.

"It's why *I'm* here," she said. "Why are you here?"

I shrugged. "Compassion. Seeing both sides."

"Like I said, fair."

The next pause was longer, itchier.

"Val," I said. "Are you in love with him?"

She shot me a glance.

"Love, more than anything, is relative," she said. "The version of me who is a character in that comfort-read of a book is in love with him, yes. The me who has been 'cured' . . . I don't know. I don't even know if I'd like him if I met him again. I don't even know if I could tolerate him, now it's clear that everything he stood for, everything he fought against was . . . bullshit. Nothing. Whatever fucking idiot nonsense he believed in with all his ferocity and passion. Guns, bivouacs, lookout detail. Val's dreams defined my world, but it was a very boy scout sort of world to dream of, don't you think?"

She ducked her head to the side. "But maybe," she said. "Maybe I want something to be real. After all that."

I nodded. That, at the very least, was something I could understand.

———————

Although we hadn't brought much with us from Ironside, we left as much as we could in the house. Leila had found a set of binoculars in one of the upstairs cupboards, a find whose serendipity she didn't see fit to question.

We didn't talk much. A new strain of silence blossomed between us, a more delicate kind I found myself tiptoeing around, even though I don't think I fully understood it. It was clearer to me now that what I imagined we had in common was little more than a narrative of my own invention. The truth was I didn't know Leila and she didn't know me, despite all the stories I'd told her, gabbling on like a schoolboy to keep the dark at bay.

We slipped out the back door of the house and followed the overgrown alleyway running behind the street. The path led circuitously behind the bland suburban backyards, meeting further, similar alleys to converge in the lee of a steep verge, with a loose baffling wall built along its crest like a fortification. Behind the wall was the old motorway, a broad blackened stripe cut deep into the landscape. The road was cut off in various places, junctions artfully blocked. This was a quiet section and the quietness felt artificial and untrustworthy. The empty road stretched into both distances like a primed trap and so we avoided it, following along on the grassy side of the verge until we reached the narrow concrete avenue of the footbridge slung high across the tarmac, like the boom mast of a sailing ship. Even from our sheltered position, I could see a mass of junk and barbed wire propped against each end of the bridge, in a slipshod attempt at a home-made defensive barrier.

We paused by a gap in the fence line, where some of the panels had blown loose. Keeping out of view of the bridge itself, Leila raised her binoculars, and I could see a look of concentration cloud her features.

"They're on the other side," she said. "Look, you can see the smoke from their bonfire. *Bonfires.*" She shook her head. "God. They've gotten careless since I left."

She traced the line of the bridge in a slow sweep.

"They have a patrol on the bridge. The walls are high, but I can see a beanie hat . . . yes, there he is. Oh bless. They've built him a lookout platform in the middle."

"Did he see you?"

"No. He's bored. A kid. He's not really looking. Old enough to take responsibility, young enough not to have anything serious to worry about."

She pulled back and sat down against the fence. She looked thoughtful; her face flushed.

"They're . . . quite well established," she said. "I mean it's a mess. But I could see fences around the place. Barbed wire, wooden stakes. They've put the hours in making it look secure."

"They've set up a compound."

"I'd say they're occupying most of the woodland. I saw some rooftops in there. What did it used to be?"

The everyday trivia of the question took me by surprise. My notion of the city's geography still hadn't quite recovered from my years of disorientation. The fixed points of its map had softened and shifted with my experience of it. Quiet suburban streets had become scavenging grounds filled with monsters, then empty gauntlets where a sniper might pick you off if you moved without care. North and south reversed themselves, gravity was upside down. A dreamlike conviction that disparate roads and neighbourhoods connected because an expediency of storytelling had edited out the parts in between.

"I think," I said, ratcheting through my rusted memory. "There was a garden centre around here somewhere?"

"A garden centre?"

"A plush one. Lots of conservatories and outbuildings. Building supplies too. A joiners, I think."

I had a memory of the place, pencil lines only. A contract job on the far side of town. Me trudging around in work gear, pushing a trolley laden with bags of cement, while around me, well-turned-out ladies from the suburbs gathered pots of brightly coloured flowers.

I could see a smile forming on Leila's face. "Fenced off. A good water supply. I can think of worse places to set up camp."

"They had a cafe too." I remembered the chink of cups and saucers, forks and spoons as I'd passed the terrace. It was the sort of idea of "civilised" I'd resented back then but feel sentimental about now.

We watched for the best part of the morning like a pair of birders in a hide. Leila let me use the binoculars, but I saw only what she'd already described, and in some respects the view was better when she told it. It was, in effect, the outlines of someone else's story, written in an abstract that didn't quite connect with me anymore. We watched, patient and quiet. Activity in the camp was sparse—only the occasional bobbing hat moving back and forth along the bridge.

Come the afternoon, we worked our way further down the fence line, keeping out of sight until we got a better view of the turn-off from the motorway. Here, there was a heavy gate patrolled by two figures in army surplus, a large, half-demolished sign for the garden centre. The road was primed with spikes and barbed wire; the guards shifted back and forth, tracing loose ellipses on the tarmac.

"That's Cass," Leila said. "She's been there longer

than I was."

"Who's that one, there?"

Leila shrugged. "Someone new. I don't know them."

When it was my turn for the binoculars again, I tried to look past the gate and up the roadway. I could see the bubbles of festival tents set out in the car park. More figures moving around them. Men, women, children, dogs.

"There's a lot of people there." I lowered the binoculars to see Leila nodding.

"That's Val," she said, a note of pride slipping through. "There's something about him. The way he talks to people. It's like he collects them." She shot me a look, her curiosity genuine. "Did yours do the same?"

"Mine?"

"The woman you followed. Your believer."

"Yes," I said. "I think she did."

A thought occurred to me and I lowered the binoculars. Leila reached for them instinctively. I moved them out of the way, forcing her to meet my eyes instead.

"When you saw the news," I said, "what did it say?"

Leila shrugged. "Oh I don't know. It was very quick. Mostly pictures. I saw *him*. Briefly, you know. Definitely him, I thought."

"It wasn't a forecast, was it?" I said. "I thought that was the sort of thing they'd do, but they wouldn't, would they? They're trying to make everything look normal.

They're trying not to make people afraid, because that's what makes it spread. So, they're not going to report stories like this unless there's something else happening. Something they can put a positive spin on."

Leila didn't reply, she stared past me, her eyes unfocussed.

"You've thought about this already, haven't you?" I said.

"Not exactly," Leila said. "I saw pictures. Blurry pictures, like I said. But I recognised the shape of him, the way he walked. I saw Val. And I *hoped* . . ."

She turned to look at me then, a vividness to her I hadn't seen before.

"How long has the lull been going on for now?" she said.

"There is no lull," I said, "not really."

"No, but for them, they're in a lull. How long has it been?"

"I don't know, I—"

"What do you do when you stop running, Spence? What do you do when whatever it is you're running from isn't there anymore?"

She smiled. "You start to rebuild. That's what they're doing. *That's* what they were reporting on the television that day." She jabbed her finger at the gateway on the opposite side of the motorway. "They've outlasted the end of the world, and so they're preparing themselves to build a new one."

I sometimes wonder what it takes for people to consider how civilisation should be defined.

We call ourselves civilised, we look down on people we think of as less civilised, but I don't think anyone really takes the time to imagine what the term means at an empirical level. Certainly nothing beyond a certain material status. As a species, we like to rank ourselves. *We* are better than *them*; *they* have more than *us*.

Perhaps civilisation is only whatever we think of as normal, or perhaps it's the baseline normality we're born into. It's a series of expectations that shifts forward with each generation. A series of technological landmarks to tick off the list: electricity, refrigeration, the internet.

The higher we climb, the further we fall.

So, if your world had been through the sort of upheaval that knocks your definition of civilisation back several generations, what level do you aspire to rebuild to? What is the civilisation you construct from the ruins you find yourself in?

I don't know what sort of world Val imagined he would be building in his encampment off the motorway.

The infection painted over half his world, black-barring it like a censored document, so he only saw with the immediacy of the present tense. He was building a world blind to the parts that still existed, and I suppose there was a historical precedence to that.

Drama needs conflict. Val's story would have drama, I had no doubt.

Leila and I made our way back to the house for the evening. I don't know if her plan had been to infiltrate Val's camp that day, and I don't know what I would have done if she had, but something about the scale of what we'd witnessed had given her the sort of hesitation that made me relieved. When I suggested we take our time to plan and regroup, she agreed readily.

We stopped off in a small, abandoned convenience store on our way back and picked up some bottled water and various supplies from what looked like freshly stocked shelves. Leila filled a bag with fruit and vegetables that, although not quite on the turn, looked as though they'd been sitting on the counter for longer than most of the canned goods.

"I don't think I ever *saw* fruit in the old days," she said. "I guess it must have been there. Maybe their presence seemed . . . unrealistic?"

I became conscious we were passing a number of vans and trucks parked up in the streets closer to Val's compound. Most were in a state of disrepair, broken windows and missing wheels, but there was something artful about the way they were arranged that reminded me of the red van I'd been directed to when I'd first been cured. A similar sense of poise, of watchfulness; a similar sense of a breath being held.

I nodded at each van as we passed them. Whether they were populated by cameras or the armed military on surveillance detail, I was struck by a need to differentiate us from the infected. Like the man we had seen in his garden to the north of the river, I wanted it understood that I *saw* them, that I *knew* who they were. It occurred to me I was proud of being cured and that I wanted it known I could tell the difference between one story and another.

I didn't share my observations with Leila. She seemed caught up in a story of her own and I had no wish to interrupt it.

When we reached the house on Katelyn Street, we stayed in the back rooms and kept our profiles low as we prepared a simple meal in the kitchen. I set the table, making it look as grand as I could manage. Knives and forks, folded kitchen towels as serviettes, the new bottled water in wineglasses, and the best chinaware I had found in the display cupboard at the top of the stairs and which had nearly broken when I forced the door open.

"Special occasion?" Leila said.

I told her about how, when I was a kid, we would sometimes have "proper mealtimes." On the days when my parents were acting as though they were together and we were pretending to be a "real" family again. I didn't tell her how awkward and uncomfortable they had been.

"Also," I said, "I used to work in a restaurant, so."

"I thought you washed dishes."

I don't know why I should have been surprised to realise she'd been listening to my horror stories after all.

"Well," I said, "you pick up skills. That's what I'm saying."

The meal was simple. Pasta and red sauce from a jar, augmented with a few of the vegetables Leila had found, which we roasted to pulp in the oven. It was bland but hearty enough. The portions more generous than I'd become used to at Ironside.

When we were done, I raided the cupboard in the lounge and found an unopened bottle of twelve-year-old Balvenie. I cracked the seal and we took a little, mostly in silence, sitting in the lounge and watching the light fade around us.

"One thing I should tell you about Val," Leila said eventually. And then she told me everything.

6

Leila's Story

One thing I should tell you about Val, is that he was never a destination. I found myself with him, but he wasn't the flag on the horizon I steered toward. He wasn't what I was looking for, he was someone I found on the way. And sometimes that's enough. You find someone going the same direction as you are and it's all the connection you need when the world had turned as much as it had.

Otherwise, I would have rushed to have told you that Val, or people like Val, were not my type. Not in the slightest. And if I resent anything about the narrative, it's the way it fell back on such outmoded tropes as to *make* him into someone I might look at twice. But that's how it worked isn't it? That's what the doctors said. It feeds off familiar beats. Comfortable rhythms. Things we've seen a million times on TV are somehow easier to believe.

I've always surprised myself.

Past-me would be disappointed by what present-me

had become, present-me was always surprised I wasn't as disappointed as I anticipated myself to be when I got there.

When I was a kid, I told myself I would never get married, I would never have kids, I would never work in an office, I would never own a flat or a house or a car. I would live abroad, somewhere tropical. I would get a deep tan all over and I would live in a hut on a beach and every morning I would go down to the surf and swim, which would make me lean and fit and un-afraid. I would collect shells and line them up along the wall in my home. I would learn to fish. I would learn to sing. I would watch the stars come out as the day began to fade and I would listen to the curl of the ocean tide long into the night. There would be something about the isolation of it all that I was certain I would find beauty in.

I married when I was twenty-six. His name was Peter and there was an aspect about him which I simply hadn't accounted for. He taught history in the same school where I was working—temporarily, or so I imagined—as a lab technician. I was preparing the materials for each science lesson and putting them away according to the safety procedures. My role was ordering the building blocks of the world, his was ordering the things that had already happened.

I thought, as a kid, I understood how people worked

and how they acted, but here was someone—a man, of all people—who was different in a way I hadn't anticipated, and I couldn't tell you why. I still don't believe the lie we're told that there's one person out there for everyone. I don't believe for a moment in the sort of chemistry people talk about in movie reviews. I don't believe opposites necessarily or cleanly attract. Relationships aren't scientific, they're not mathematical. They're chaotic, abstract, irrational.

Peter was the opposite of Val. He was lean and small. Funny and smart. Geeky, silly, sweet. But despite all of that, there was an aspect of him that *fitted* into an aspect of me—not biological, not chemical. Something else, something... different, unquantifiable. And for a moment, I suppose I did believe in all the silly nonsense I thought I wouldn't.

But then.

I got pregnant early in our marriage. A mistake, a surprise, a gift that sent us scurrying to our numbers to see if we could afford to live as three people rather than two. We were frightened, then excited, then terrified it might not happen. All that spent worry, all for nothing.

But it did happen. *He* happened. It was a difficult labour, then at three in the morning, Jamie was born. I was exhausted, every part of me felt as though it was rubbing against something serrated and cruel, but the doc-

tors met me with smiles. *He* was fit and healthy, I was assured. A lively child. A bouncing, baby boy.

And as I held him for the first time, still aching with
the pain of him, I saw he was small, red, already furious
with the world. I asked myself when I would know, without any doubt or duty, that I loved him.

Love is something we're told mothers have fitted as
standard. An instinct to protect the young. Momma
bears and momma lions and momma sharks and seals.
We see it on every nature documentary, we see it on
every soap opera, in every romantic novel, on every news
cycle and sitcom and advert for life insurance.

I waited for that love to come. This little boy, this
strange little man. Screaming and screaming at me, sap-
ping the life from me by degrees. I waited, and while I
waited, I gave all I had to him, *investing* in him because . . .
I thought that was how it was supposed to work. You paid
for things you would love and cherish and keep and nur-
ture and . . .

But each night, when he finally slept, I lay awake, terrified he would wake up. Terrified he wouldn't. And the
day would start again, and in some ways, it would be a
relief because then I knew how . . . *awful* he was. I didn't
have to doubt myself while he was there with me, taking
and taking and taking . . .

And every news article I read told me I was a Bad

Mother. And everything I saw on the television reminded me how I should be Ashamed of Myself. And every look passing strangers gave me on the street was poisoned, as I pushed his screaming self from street corner to street corner. Every story I read confirmed—if not outright, then at least by implication—that *I* was the monster, not him. Me, because something expected was missing.

It'd be easy to say Peter let all of this happen, that he neglected us both—that's how these stories normally go, isn't it? And, god, it would make it so much easier if it was his fault. But it wasn't. But he didn't. He was a good man, for pity's sake, and I would even hazard a guess he really did understand when he told me he did. Even if my first instinct was to recoil from the suggestion, as though his empathy was trespassing on my own personal pain. Silently, without argument, he gave me room. He cut down his work hours, took over more and more of the childcare, the cooking, the housework. He took Jamie on trips in the car, slackening the tautness of responsibility so I could have hours and days to myself.

We didn't talk about it. That was a problem: we each assumed the other's motives. We *understood*, but we didn't interrogate, we didn't look for ways to solve. Peter and I put on this act together, a dramatic performance of Everything's Just Fine. Fixed smiles and familiar motions.

We put it on so long we kept the performance up even when we were alone together. We both knew how I was *supposed* to act. The books, the papers, the television had hammered it into us both and I don't think either of us once entertained the idea it might not always be true.

I wonder.

I wonder if I started to resent Jamie then because he was taking Peter away from me as well? I wonder if I allowed myself to become jealous of him because that was a motive I could at least understand? I wonder if I was frightened of him, even then, before anything happened.

Jamie was nearly six when the world started to break. When people on the news started acting crazy, when everyone was sharing videos of madness on the streets, when there was talk of the dead coming back to life.

"Perhaps," Peter said, "we should turn this off." He meant the news or the television or the outside world or all of it. I know he was speaking on Jamie's behalf. He didn't want to frighten him; he didn't want the boy to see us afraid. Peter had an understanding of how stories could be infectious, I suppose. History is one long string of stories honed to sharpen one side over another.

But it still felt needling at the time. Patronising in a way I know it wasn't intended to be.

"Perhaps we should stop watching," he said, and all I heard was, "You're in no fit state to deal with any of this."

The world ended late in the morning of a lazy Saturday, and by three that afternoon I had murdered my son and my husband and fled the house we called our home.

In one version of the story, the disease took Jamie first. I was in the kitchen, washing the dishes with more care than they needed because it took more time. An adult task during which I could not be disturbed. The radio was loud in an act of defiance. The news was on, feeding me outrage and horror.

I heard my son coming down the stairs and I knew something had changed. The movement *sounded* wrong to me. It sounded as though something ungainly was dragging itself, step after step. There was a low moaning sound, an asthmatic quality to the way each breath was taken. I called Jamie's name and then edged to the doorway to look into the hall.

Whatever I saw, I swear to you it was not my son. It was not my baby boy.

In his place, there was a monster, a thing, an *Other*. A wet, red hand clasping the ball at the end of the banister rail, supporting the weight of it as it lurched into view. Its face was a bloody horror of decay and disease. Its eyes were empty holes. At first, I didn't even recognise it as having once been my son. The details that alerted me were material. Clothing I had bought with the household income: the spaceman T-shirt, the khaki shorts, the blue buckle sandals. All were now as stained and rotten as the beast who wore them. It's absurd that my first thought was *it's wearing Jamie's clothes!* But for the first time in our life spent together, I was afraid for Jamie. What if this *thing* had caused him harm? I screamed his name and the creature kept coming toward me.

I called for Peter who I'd last seen going upstairs to the bedroom. When I got no response, I ran back to the kitchen to arm myself against the creature stumbling toward me. I spilled the drawers—knives and rolling pins and carving forks skittered across the floor. The thing was on me then, wailing, baring bloodied teeth.

I shoved it away and it crumpled against the kitchen cabinet. Its lightness, its *delicacy* surprising me as I rushed past it to the staircase.

Upstairs, I searched the bedrooms, calling Peter's name, Jamie's.

The sheets of our bed were bright red and dishevelled, dragged to the floor at the far side by the window. I edged around the room until Peter came into view, lying on the carpet, his hand still clutching the covers that had fallen with him.

His throat was gone, his chest opened, his eyes wide and emptying.

If I screamed, it was because the sight of him like that confirmed everything I thought I knew. The boy was a monster; he, *it*, would murder us all. The story was set, its dimensions locked around me.

When I rushed from the room, Jamie was there. Hollering and howling, his hands little claws. I shoved him away from me again and the stairs did the rest. A rag doll crumpled against the wall in the lower hallway after its maiden flight.

There was another roar from behind me and Peter reared up. Not Peter, something rotten puppetting what was left of him. He swung toward me but I ran, tumbling down the stairs myself, but using the speed, using the adrenaline to right myself. I stepped over the body of the little monster at the foot of the stairs without a single thought beyond thanking whoever was looking out for me for ensuring it wasn't a threat anymore. I grabbed the car keys and was starting the engine when Peter was back. Standing in front of the car like a scarecrow.

God help me. God forgive me. He didn't block my way for very long.

7

Later that night, I left Leila curled up on the armchair and went through the house like a thief. I returned to the lounge with the rest of the bottle of Balvenie and a packet of sedatives I'd found in one of the bedside drawers. Leila regarded my finds with a flat expression.

"Fuck off," she said eventually. "I'm not a doctor, but I'm ninety percent certain you're not supposed to mix those."

"You need to sleep," I said. "When was the last time you got any rest?"

She reached past the pills and took the bottle of Scotch, popping the cork with the edge of her thumb.

"Awad prescribed me pills as well," she said. "Little pink bastards rattling around in a paper cup. I told him he could fuck off too."

"Then I'm in good company." I set the box on the coffee table.

"You going to get me a glass or are you expecting me to neck from the bottle again?"

"I'll get you a glass."

I got us both a glass and Leila poured out two gener-ous measures.

"Pills and booze and bellyaches." She sat back in the armchair, chin high. "Anyone would think you were try-ing to make me forget."

"Me?"

"You, Awad, everyone else. You know what I really hate about being cured? Everyone's so ... fucking smug, you know? First thing I get when I got to the facility: It's all okay! The world isn't ending! It's make-believe, and you? Well, you fell for it because you're ... weak, or stu-pid, or angry. You're *susceptible*, that's what you are."

She threw her hands up. "Good news, it's not your fault. Bad news, you didn't narrowly escape from your husband and son who had turned into ravenous zombies, you *murdered* them both in cold blood because ... *fairy tales*. But as I said, good news!"

She shook her head. "And they say it like they think I'll see it as a happy ending. You're cured. *Boom*. It's over. But it's not over, it's worse, it's so much worse. It would have been a happy ending if they'd gone and ... I dunno, gunned us all down. Eradicate the story that way instead."

"Leila."

"I can't help imagining what really happened, that night. Not what *I* saw. What ... Jamie must have seen. Did he see me as a monster? Was that why he hid behind the banister at the foot of the stairs? Was I already acting in a way that frightened him?

"And it's just . . . it sounds childish, but it's not fair. It proved everyone right. I *was* the monster. Not because of what I did at the end, but because of the way I couldn't connect with him before. And I wanted to, I wanted to more than anything in the whole world, but I *couldn't*. And then this disease, this *narrative* came along and it made matters even worse and . . . how was I supposed to get out of that? How was I supposed to make it better? How could I have done things differently with the odds so cruelly stacked? There was no way. No way."

She swallowed hard and swigged the whiskey like beer. She sniffed and sat back. I topped up her glass.

"It wasn't fair," she said again. "If things hadn't gone the way they had, I would have learned to love him. I only needed time. We were getting closer, I'm sure of it. And now he's gone, I miss him so much. Pete too, but . . . Jamie?"

She closed her eyes.

"When I was infected, when I was running with Val and the rest. No one questioned that I'd lost them. Everyone had lost someone, someone close. It was something we all thought we had in common. And there was me, a mother who had lost her husband and six-year-old son to the disease. I told people I loved them more than anything in the whole world and I swear to you it was *true*. There was nothing I was more certain of in my life.

"But now.

"Now I don't know if that was true or some part of the narrative. Part of the story."

She fell silent; blindly reaching for the glass, she knocked it with the tip of her finger and it fell to the carpet.

"It's alright." I replaced her glass with mine and fished hers from the rug, where the stain of liquid had blossomed and spread across the fibres of the carpet.

"You asked before how I got cured," she said. "I was so stupid. I was out on a supply raid. Val was there, I wonder if things would have been different if he hadn't been. There was an accident, we were out at one of the places by the river. There were . . . *Others* there, we could smell them, we could see shapes moving about. The lull had made us brave, I suppose. Or stupid. One of the two. Anyway, these poor saps must have been hiding in the basement from us, when I stepped out onto the floor above them and it fell through. Me with it. The roof had been leaking and the floorboards were completely rotted. Took me by surprise.

"I landed badly, fucked up my leg. And of course, Val and some of his lieutenants step up to the edge to look down and see me down there surrounded by Others.

Well, you can imagine how that looks. Anyway, he picks them off, one by one. Headshots. Pop, pop, pop. But he doesn't come down. He doesn't help.

"'You got to kill her too,' someone says. 'She's been bitten. Look at her.' But he doesn't. He gives me a hard look. Lots of stuff going on in there but he doesn't say a damn thing to me. He just holsters his handgun and fucks off. His buddies follow."

She shrugged.

"Getting 'bitten' is the worst way to get cured," she said. "Because of course you think you're going to turn and you're afraid. But in reality, the actual pain of getting injured . . . wakes you up, I suppose. You don't change, that's clear. Maybe the narrative can't work properly at a biological level. You see your legs have been ripped up by teeth, but your pain receptors are telling you something else. The friction between the real and the perceived becomes . . . *tiresome*, ill-fitting. The narrative feels trivial. So, it's self-preservation that makes you refocus, so you can deal with your own injuries.

"So that's how I was cured," she said. "I got hurt, then got left behind. Then, eventually, I thought, 'I don't want to play this game anymore.' Only . . ."

She closed her eyes and fell into silence.

"Only . . . it's funny. I miss being infected," she said.

"I'm sorry?"

139

"I *miss* being infected. I miss the narrative." Her smile was small, her eyes raw. "Not because of Val, never because of him. No, I miss the certainty of it. It made the world so . . . simple. It was us and them and that was that. The whole world was black and white. Everything was easy. And most important of all, I loved my son with such a ferocity it lit a fire within me and that fire fuelled me in the way nothing else could.

"I miss *missing* him in that way. I miss loving him so unconditionally. I miss him and I miss the disease that made me see monsters."

Her hand moved to her face. Her eyes clenched shut.

I waited until her breathing steadied before I spoke.

"Do you want to go back?" I said.

She looked at me, she nodded.

"More than anything," she said.

I said at the beginning when I tell this story, I tell people it's a love story. The version of the story I tell on those occasions is—as you might have anticipated—an edited version. It's not often I get the luxury to sit in company such as this and tell absolutely everything. How long have I been talking now? Have we missed lunch already?

Your attention flatters me.

But maybe I'm wrong. Maybe a love story is barely a love story at all when its machinery lies so exposed.

Despite that, I feel it necessary to underline that what happened next, happened absolutely out of love. It happened out of respect and compassion. It might even, I hope, result in a positive outcome for all of us: the infected and the cured and the immune. Although I don't think I've ever been guilty of hubris before, I hold onto that idea. In the nights that followed I held onto the thought as a glimmer of hope on my long road home.

Look. I'm not a doctor, I've taken no Hippocratic oath, but even then, I'm well aware of—let's say—the *ethical* implications of what I did that night in the house on Katelyn Street. I'm fully aware of how cynical it must seem to so deliberately try to reinfect someone who was cured. Even if there was consent on her part, let's be very clear: I was a man, gaslighting a woman. I was lying to her to send her back to a violent life because . . . well. I wish there was a way of finishing that sentence easily. I wish I could justify myself with complete confidence. I can't, acknowledging only how we live in strange and unpredictable times.

I'm not proud.

And all it took was for me to tell her a story.

———————

Of course, there were aspects of Leila's own story that were familiar to me.

Of all the recollections I'd heard during my time running with Macey and the rest, of all the stories I've heard since being cured, during group sessions very much like this one, the most common was where the narrators related how they witnessed members of their own family transforming into an Other and giving chase.

Have you noticed how these sorts of stories always end in betrayal?

Mine's no different.

In the stories you hear, lovers, husbands, wives, mothers, fathers, kids become irrevocably changed; parental instincts are subverted, childish dependencies are corrupted. Many of the "survivors" telling the stories simply escaped their homes, fleeing the monsters they thought their loved ones had become. But there are those—like Leila—who fought back, often to lethal effect.

"It wasn't really them," these survivors would tell me by way of explanation, while we gathered around the campfire out in the wilderness, exchanging anecdotal evidence to legitimise one another. "It wasn't the person I loved. Not anymore."

And *there* would be the licence to do the harm that had, perhaps, always been dreamed of.

The narrative was strengthened by stories about those

who hadn't fled from their loved ones in this way. Those who became infected or were devoured because they couldn't accept the "truth." One kid I met told me how he and his sister saw their newly monstrous parents lurching toward them across the garden. The boy's name was Kir and he had implored his sister that she shouldn't let them back in the house. He begged her, telling her they should both run away, but she'd ignored him and unlatched the kitchen door, stepping forward willingly to be embraced by the creatures.

Kir told me how he'd been powerless to stop her, he told me she wouldn't listen to his reason, and instead he'd watched in horror as they fed upon her in front of him. He saw her go limp in their arms. She had given him the room he needed to escape, he said, and he spoke of her often as though her sacrifice was something he still needed to earn and atone for. He told me the last he'd seen of his sister had been her rotting face at the window, watching him flee.

But now, of course, we all know the truth was very different. Did his sister simply accept what she saw? Or did she refuse to believe the story her infection fed to her. Had her own physical reality proved the lie of the narrative? Was it really as simple as physical coercion which proved her parents weren't monsters? Was it something as intangible as familial love that broke down the horrors she'd imagined?

How satisfying, how *humiliating* to think the cure had always been so easily within our grasp. Kept distant from us by our own cynicism, our own jaundiced conviction that strength lay in complexity, in convolution.

The believers kept us blind to this understanding. I certainly couldn't see Macey buying it. *Perhaps we all just need a hug*, was never going to cut it. If my own family come stumbling toward me on a stormy day, I would have run a mile had they appeared to be infected or not.

To her credit, when it came to the Others, Macey always preferred avoidance over confrontation, but if anyone under her wing got too close, she would be swift to excommunicate them for the safety of everyone else. She could be ruthless, unapologetic in her betrayals, in the same way I imagined Val to be.

———————

Macey wouldn't approve, but I've been dreaming a lot recently.

Or at least, I've been remembering my dreams more. Awad once suggested the simple act of recalling my dreams might be evidence of the cure cementing itself. Proof the narrative is shaking loose. His theory is that our dreams serve a facility to work through our perception of different realities and the narrative shuts them down as though they represent a form of competition. I don't know. Sometimes I worry it's my unbidden way of trying to reconstruct the narrative I already lost.

It's a problem I have these days. Stories are addictive. I keep imagining futures for the world. I keep imagining I had a part in them, no matter how small.

And then, I suppose, you could say I wake up and I see my place in relation to everything else is tiny, insignificant, mostly known for having followed the straightest path without thought and done harm to others.

My favourite dreams are the ones in which I'm forgiven. I wonder if it's because I always wake from them a moment before they turn sour.

I dream of how Leila's reinfection might look to Val and his crew. To them, she'd have been "infected" and now she'd be seen as "cured," the familiar terminology subverted and confounded by perspective. When you think of people who have survived an illness like this, what do you imagine? Cures, vaccines, ways forward and out of the maze? I wonder how Val's crew would treat her. If they were—as Leila had insisted—trying to establish civilisation on their own terms, then perhaps her return would spur them to investigate their own solution? How would they be if the narrative shifted to accommodate the idea they might somehow, magically, cure themselves?

If Val *believed* he found a cure as part of the narrative, then his followers would believe as well. What (my dream self asks) would happen then? Where would it lead? Would their definition of *cured* be the same as the one we now understood, or would it be another layer of fiction, another division? Would they inflict their cure on those of us they came across? Or would they come to see us as though we'd been saved by their hand? Would they start seeing the world differently, looking for signs that the Others were people again?

I dream of Val's civilisation; I imagine it built of rusting metal and repurposed detritus meeting the remains of the old world, which has endured despite itself. Two distinct sides, each of which think they're the ones responsible for saving everyone. Each can only pretend to understand their counterpart, but here they are, rubbing up against one another, creating conflicting narratives of their own.

We have moved forward. We have moved onward to turn a corner thought impassable. New problems, new narratives have flowered in our path, but these will be for better minds than mine to resolve.

My greatest sin and my greatest achievement are the same. I told a story.

I told it the way Macey taught me. I told it to Leila, first in hypothetical terms. Imagine, I said, how Val and his gang would see this story we're going to make you be-lieve. Put yourself in their shoes. What would it take for them to let you to come home?

"Home," she had said, using the word as though it was alien to her, as though its context had become twisted into something that felt ill-fitting of her own experience.

"We have to make you believe in that word again," I said.

We stayed up late into the night in the house on Kate-lyn Street, spinning elaborate tales. I pulled things back, kept things simple. We don't need to know the science behind it, I said. If we complicate it, it'll be harder to believe.

"For them?" Leila said.

"For you," I said.

Over and over, I told her story, iterating as I went. Re-drafting it, editing it, strengthening it, making it tough and sinewy. I told it as Leila got drunker and I told it as she fell asleep. I shifted the vocabulary, tenses changed from past to present, perspective shifted to second per-son, to first. I told the story long into the night, whisper-ing it, repeating it, making it gospel, making it real, so it crowbarred its way into her memory through the door-way of her dreams.

Macey would've been proud of me.

I hope Macey would've been proud of me.

8

This is what happened.

Leila was injured during a routine supply raid. She fell through the rotten wooden floorboards of a warehouse near the river and fractured her tibia. She landed in the basement, where a group of uninfected residents had been hiding from the violence of the raiding party.

Val responded to her cry, but he stood in the safety of the room's doorway and shot and killed the "Others" he imagined were trying to attack her. He then left her there without a word, assuming she was beyond help, not willing to be the one to kill her himself. It transpired his cowardice had always been as selective as his heroism.

Leila survived anyway, and by the time she encountered an uninfected reconnaissance party stealthily surveying the south bank of the river, the strength of the narrative had begun to wane, and she was capable of understanding they were there to help her. They took her to a hospital in the north, and from there to Ironside, where the full impact of the cure sent her spiralling.

This is what happened.

Val saw when you fell. You lay on the floor in that basement, the pain thundering through you and you saw him run into the room above, framed in the ragged hole of broken floorboards. You saw a look of panic in him that was new. As though it was his foundations that had been undercut and not yours.

When he saw you, he faltered, his weapon drawn but not aimed. You could hear the footsteps of the survivors on the raid, you could hear the stuttering breaths of Others, lurking in the darkness around you, but you surprised yourself by not being afraid. For that brief moment it felt as though you and Val were alone.

"Stay strong," Val said, his voice quiet, insistent, focussed, meant only for you. But this was not an order, he was pleading with you. "Please," he said, "Fight this."

Figures appeared in the doorway behind him, and when he raised the gun, you almost believed he might be aiming at you, as though this was the kindness you had always known of him.

The shots sang as the monsters fell and then you were alone and it felt like a promise.

This is what happened.

Val. Listen to me. I was attacked, I was bitten, but I didn't change. Not like everyone else did. I was found in the basement, they took me to a laboratory and they put me on display.

The doctors said they'd never seen anything like it before. No one they knew had been infected but survived. White coats in white walled rooms. *Immune* they said, and they said it like an incantation. It didn't feel like science, it felt like prayer.

This was why they wouldn't leave me alone.

This was why they kept me in their little cell.

This was why they kept running their stupid, stupid tests.

Only we can heal the world, they said. Only we can make it whole.

But I swear to you they won't be happy until they've blended me down to a smoothie they can share in the break room.

I never asked for this. I have never claimed to be special; I only want my life to be normal, easy. A world I can face each day without being overwhelmed with anxiety.

You're never going to let me leave here, are you, I said to them. And they smiled at me from behind their goggles and hairnets and rubber gloves.

When we're done here, they said, they'll build statues

in your honour.

I want to go home, I said. I don't want a statue.

Everybody wants a statue, they said. They approached with needles. Keep still now, they said. Still as a statue. Stiller.

I plotted my escape. I befriended another inmate. An older guy, ugly as sin but clear enough he'd seen a few things. This was a laboratory rather than a prison, so it was not as secure as the white coats imagined. We nearly got caught in the final push, but my friend laid out the guard who came at us and sent him flying, shattering a window.

Strange how that made me smile. It reminded me how we used to think that anything was possible if we set our minds to it.

We fled across the river, running homeward. For a few days, it was like old times. The freedom of the outside, the wind at our backs and the sun on our faces. We were away from the laboratory for barely moments and already it was fading from me like a dream.

In a house in the south suburbs, we were attacked and my friend was bitten. He was not immune like they tell me I am, but still, he didn't attack me. He stayed back and let me go, that thousand-yard stare corrupted but clear, his expression contrite.

I walked the final path alone.

Val, I've come home.
Val. I stayed strong. I fought.
Val. I'm here.

———————

That night, Leila slept in a way I hadn't been aware of during the short time I had known her. The loaded silence was replaced with a restlessness familiar to me from other residents of Ironside. She didn't talk in her sleep but she subvocalised, the murmurs, groans, and sighs of a dreamer in their most natural state. I left a blanket over her in the armchair and moved quietly to the kitchen, searching the drawers until I found a first aid kit in one and a chef's knife in another.

I hid the first aid kit in the bread bin and waited in the kitchen until the dawn began to edge across the room with a ripening brightness. Then I took the knife and cut open the sleeve of my shirt, tracing a line across the back of the arm beneath it, enough for the blood to bubble outward; a thickening barbed thread like a thorny acacia branch, it swelled then succumbed to gravity, rolling down my arm in a series of long fingers as the pain sharpened me fully into wakefulness.

I dropped the knife behind the countertop, and unlatched the backdoor, trailing blood artfully, my head already lightening. I waited until the blood had soaked into the sleeve of my shirt before I planted my elbow roughly through the lower glass pane of the door and kicked the woodwork so it slammed open against the outer wall.

Leila was awake and in the kitchen, her eyes bulbous.

She took in the scene I had contrived in an instant, but I watched her eyes, looking for the spark.

"Someone broke in," I said. "Some guy . . . I think there was something wrong with him."

I laughed, self-deprecating.

"He was crazy," I said. "All clawed fingers and gnashing teeth . . ."

An old story from a different time. But what if it was real? What if Val and Macey and everyone else were right? She lifted my arm and peeled back the ragged cloth to reveal the clean line of the wound I had made. She held my hand in hers for a moment, her face hidden from me as I held my breath, partly because the pain hammered at me, partly because I was afraid of what she saw. If she saw only a knife wound, then it had been for nothing.

But when she looked up at me, there was more than tears in her eyes. There was something else, something bright and sharp and terribly familiar.

"Spence," she said.

"I'm alright." I'm no actor but I knew I didn't sound alright.

Her head turned slowly; her eyes closed tight.

"No," she said. "No. You're not."

You can imagine the scene; you've probably seen it yourself a hundred times. Tears, cries, screams against the injustice of the world. And I told her to go on without me, to go to Val's place, to save the world. That sort of thing.

My betrayal.

She believed.

After she'd left, I bound up my wound with the gauze and disinfectant I'd set aside, then gathered my own belongings and followed her at a distance. I found her hesitating at the entrance to the footbridge over the freeway. I heard multiple voices, rising in argument. I hid near the gap of the baffling fence and watched the trace of movement as people rushed back and forth behind the concrete walls. There was a hum and a buzz to the encampment; quite at odds with the watchful quiet I'd sensed of it the day before.

I stayed long into the following night, listening for the sound of gunshots that might curtail the story I'd curated before it had time to fully ripen.

When I was certain none would come, I turned my back on the camp, I turned my back on Leila, and I started my journey home.

9

I didn't come home straight away. You know that. I came back here only last week and you're right, at least a year or two has passed since I last saw some of you.

By *home*, of course, I mean here, Ironside, the facility, this lounge, everyone. The word had an easier fit for me than it ever did for Leila, but it struck me that Ironside was for those who believed they were cured, those who—as Awad keeps telling us—were infected through no fault of their own.

To me, I didn't think it was right to come back, alone and at fault, and assume to be treated with the respect and the kindness I had come to expect of the place. A simple absolution was something I believe I'd forfeited. I made a choice instead to abdicate myself from the world. My next journey would be low impact, intended only to scrape away the footprints I'd already left behind.

I took a long way home. I took the deck of photographs from my pocket and spread them out like a map. I took the most scenic of routes.

During my last months in Ironside, Awad had set me

up with Clancy from the reconciliation department and together we'd looked up names and addresses of everyone I killed in that restaurant fire and those I had killed since whose names I still remembered. The list is hopelessly incomplete, but it was enough to give me purpose. With those documents in my hand, I walked the region. South of the river, the north. The inner suburbs, the islands. I rang doorbells, knocked on windows, I told people who I was and what I'd done. I saw their faces turn white, then red. I saw anger, grief, agonising calm.

A young man in the capital's inner suburbs chased me around three blocks, shouting cuss words at me before he broke down in a doorway and let me carry him home. An elderly lady up in the north invited me into her kitchen and made me eat cake and drink heavily sugared tea. She showed me photographs of her daughter and her grandson, and when I had to remind her what I'd done to them, she smiled, understanding only what she needed to and ignoring the rest.

"I know," she said. "I wanted to show you them as they really were."

I went to visit where Macey's father had lived. I followed a trail of clues, sifted from our conversations, until they came sharply into focus. I found the house, but the man himself was long gone. He'd lived out in the suburbs to the south, and although apparently uninfected, he refused to be relocated because he was afraid his garden would run rampant without him. A band of survivors had taken him out. A clean shot through his eye while he'd been weeding the pumpkins. His body hadn't been retrieved for nearly nine months.

I went to visit where Leila had lived. A pilgrimage of sorts, I suppose. In this case, the debt was a harder metric to quantify. I stood outside the house, a modern unit of the same design as its neighbours in the street. It didn't look like the crime scene she'd described to me. I gave it a good few hours before moving on.

There's a story in each of these meetings, more to them than I've told you here, but—for now—these are my stories, my penance, and I need to hold on to them longer and closer. There'll be time for them one day, maybe, but not today.

I'm sure you understand.

I was never seeking forgiveness. Awad will tell me I never need to, because it was never *me*, it was the disease and so on and so forth, but forgiveness—while something I admit I occasionally dream of—is not a blessing I feel entitled to, let alone one I expect.

I think I wanted my people to understand I knew exactly what it was I'd done. I wanted them to know *I knew* what I was responsible for, and I promised them each I would carry that understanding with me as long as I'm here to do so.

It will not bring their families back, but I hope they'll find it serves as a conclusion, because stories deserve a proper conclusion, even if they do not—cannot—have a happy ending.

So, I took the long path, and now I'm home.

I'm back at Ironside, back in the room at the end of the corridor, back with Sizemore, my neighbour, tossing and turning every night as though nothing of note has changed since I've been away.

I have done terrible things. Things that *are* absolutely my fault, but which, thanks to the Compassion Directives, I will not be punished for. Instead, I'm welcomed home again. A prodigal son, forgiven without a chance to learn from what I've done wrong.

The world is exactly as it was and I suppose there's comfort to that, isn't there? As though no matter how far you go, there's always this place, this fulcrum you can simply return to.

Home. Or something like it. I don't know.

But it does get me thinking. As I lie awake in my bed at night, barely daring to breathe in case I might mistake the sound of myself for *something* that might make my heart quicken and my mouth turn dry.

I became Leila's believer. It was a role I took upon myself; a believer who didn't believe. A Typhoid Mary of the narrative, forcing it to evolve, to double back, to knot itself into fanciful arabesques. A flicker of doubt, and the story diverges like a new shoot on a tangled vine.

Spence the Believer. It's not a role I wear with pride. It pricks at me, makes me itch so I can't keep still.

Why do you suppose it was *this* narrative that took hold and not something else? Why believe the dead were coming back to life? Did the same narrative infect everyone around the world, or was it localised? Are other countries, other *cultures*, in thrall to the same delusions we faced? Did our . . . I don't know . . . *cultural dominance* force the same stories on them at the expense of their own? Or is everyone caught up in their own fictions, born of their own histories, their own conversations, their own media?

I wonder what happened with Val and Leila and the cure they might have cultivated. How long will it take for the results of their cure to reach fruition, to spark a resurgence in the conflict between the people who see one outcome and the people who see something else.

Most of all, I try not to sleep.

Because I'm happy here. With a room of my own, with my friends and our shared experiences. I'm happy to be with people who care, who want to know, who hang on every word.

What if *this* is my new narrative? All of us here in our

cosy little haven? What if we've simply succumbed to a different, more benign story, with Awad as our believer? What if our very idea of what "being cured" means is wrong, and that rather than turning the signal off, we've done little more than to change the channel?

Or maybe we're each trapped in our own narratives and blind to the experience of everyone else? What if right now, I'm sitting alone in an abandoned building, talking to a circle of empty chairs?

What if I was to wake up in the morning and find it all gone, all a dream?

And so, I lie here instead, trying to hold off sleeping because every time I wake, I have to pinch myself to make sure that what I *believe* is real, is real still. That what I've grown to love above everything else hasn't been taken away from me. And there's a silence to me which wasn't there before. As though it was something Leila passed on like an infection of her own as we parted that final time.

But eventually, of course, I succumb to sleep. I'm not as young as I used to be. I get tired. We all get tired, and eventually I sleep along with everyone else.

And then I wake up and across the room from me, Leila says: "I don't want to be back with Val, we should keep walking. We should go onward and never look back."

We're in the house on Katelyn Street and I nod and

rub my eyes and I'm about to reply, but she smiles at me and says, "I didn't mean to wake you, Spence. Go on now. It's okay. It can wait."

And then I wake up and Macey is still asleep across the campfire from me. Her face is relaxed in her own dream, her mouth slightly open. The light through the trees softens the edges of her and makes her an angel.

And then I wake up and I'm cold and alone and from somewhere, I can hear yesterday's rain sluice down from the leaves, a secondary rainfall from the forest canopy. I huddle deep under the tarp, pressing my cheek against the coolness of the mud. I close my eyes.

And then I wake up and Sizemore is hammering on the door and calling my name.

And then I wake up and Macey is sitting at the foot of the bed. She doesn't turn to me, and her voice sounds distant when she speaks. "Long day today, Spence," she says. "Can't dawdle."

And then I wake up and there's gunfire and Val is bursting through the door, there's a machine gun cradled in his arms and his eyes are gleaming.

And then I wake up and someone is crying in the room beside mine.

And then I wake up and there's silence. Darkness.

And then I wake up and this is the love story I always wanted it to be.

And then I wake up and this, *this* is what happened.
And then I wake up.
And then.
And then.

Acknowledgements

An enormous thank-you to Ellen Datlow, Emily Gold-man, Irene Gallo, Sanaa Ali-Virani, Ruoxi Chen, and all at Tordotcom. It's been an absolute dream and I'm pinching myself for the opportunity you've afforded me.

Thank you Stephen Graham Jones, Mira Grant, Nancy Kress, Alma Katsu, Brian Evenson, and Kaaron Warren for your extraordinary generosity.

Thank you also to Helen Marshall, Kelly Sandoval, Usman Malik, Hugo Xiong, and Nina Allan for reading early versions of the story, which would not be a thing at all without your input.

About the Author

Malcolm Devlin's stories have appeared in *Black Static, Interzone, The Shadow Booth,* and *Shadows and Tall Trees.* His first collection, *You Will Grow Into Them,* was published by Unsung Stories in 2017 and shortlisted for the British Fantasy and Saboteur Awards. A second collection, *Unexpected Places to Fall From, Unexpected Places to Land,* was published by Unsung Stories in 2021. He currently lives in Brisbane.

TOR·COM

Science fiction. Fantasy. The universe.

And related subjects.

*

More than just a publisher's website, *Tor.com* is a venue for **original fiction, comics,** and **discussion** of the entire field of SF and fantasy, in all media and from all sources. Visit our site today—and join the conversation yourself.